ACQUIRED BY
HER GREEK BOSS

BY
CHANTELLE SHAW

MILLS &
BOON

First Published in Great Britain 2017
By Mills & Boon, an imprint of HarperCollins*Publishers*
1 London Bridge Street, London, SE1 9GF

© 2017 Chantelle Shaw

ISBN: 978-0-263-92399-5

Printed and bound in Spain
by CPI, Barcelona

Alekos wa... might be her only opportunity to meet her blood relations. Common sense doused her excitement. 'It would look strange if you took your PA to a private engagement.'

'Possibly, but you wouldn't be there as my PA. You would accompany me as my date. My mistress,' he explained, when she stared at him uncomprehendingly.

For a third time Sara's heart jolted against her ribs. 'We agreed to forget about the kiss we shared last night.' She flushed, hating how she'd sounded breathless when she had intended her voice to be cool and crisp.

His eyes gleamed like hot coals for a second, before the fire in those dark depths was replaced by the faintly cynical expression that Sara was more used to seeing.

'I don't remember agreeing to forget about it,' he drawled. 'But I'm suggesting that we *pretend* to be in a relationship. If people believe you are my girlfriend it will seem perfectly reasonable for you to be with me.'

Chantelle Shaw lives on the Kent coast and thinks up her stories while walking on the beach. She has been married for over thirty years and has six children. Her love affair with reading and writing Mills & Boon stories began as a teenager, and her first book was published in 2006. She likes strong-willed, slightly unusual characters. Chantelle also loves gardening, walking and wine!

Visit the Author Profile page at millsandboon.co.uk for more titles.

ACQUIRED BY
HER GREEK BOSS

For Pippa Roscoe,
Thank you for being a wonderful editor,
for giving great advice, for the laughs we've shared
and your understanding (and occasional tear-mopping)
when I've struggled with a book!
Best wishes always,
Chantelle

CHAPTER ONE

'CAN I HELP YOU?' Alekos Gionakis said curtly, when he strode into his office on Monday morning and found an unknown woman making coffee with his espresso machine.

In the past month he'd had four temporary PAs, all of whom had proved inadequate to the task of organising his hectic schedule. But this morning his super-efficient personal assistant was due back at work after her holiday and Alekos was looking forward to his life running smoothly again. The idea that Sara might have delayed her return for some reason, and he would have to manage for even one more day with yet another temp, cast a dark cloud over his mood.

His rapier glance skimmed over the woman's hair that fell in loose waves around her shoulders and seemed to encompass every shade of brown from caramel to latte. Her delightfully curvaceous figure was packaged in a dusky pink blouse and a cream pencil skirt that was a good two inches shorter than knee length.

Moving his gaze lower, Alekos felt a jolt of mascu-line appreciation at her shapely legs, which were en-hanced by her high-heeled shoes with cut-out sections at the front that revealed her bare toes. He noticed her toenails were varnished a flirty shade of hot pink that was more suited to a beach than to Gionakis Enterprises' prestigious offices in Piccadilly.

'Good morning, Alekos.'

He frowned at the sound of the familiar voice. Low-toned and melodious, for some reason it made him think of a cool, clear mountain stream.

'Sara?' Her *voice* was recognisable, but everything about his PA's appearance was definitely not. His brain was not playing tricks on him, Alekos realised when she turned her head. Even though she was standing several feet away from him, he was struck by the intense green of her eyes. They were her only remarkable features—or at least that had been true when Sara's style of workwear for the past two years had been a navy blue skirt and jacket, which she'd teamed with a plain white shirt, buttoned primly all the way up to her throat in the summer, or a black roll-neck sweater in colder weather.

Smart, practical and frankly unnoticeable was how Alekos would have described his PA's appearance before she had inconveniently decided to take a month's holiday in Spain. When he'd objected, she had reminded him that she hadn't used any of her annual leave since she'd started working for him, apart from one day to attend her mother's funeral. Sara had looked even more washed out than she usually did. Alekos was not renowned for his sensitivity, but he'd acknowledged that caring for her terminally ill mother must have been a strain and he'd reluctantly agreed to her taking an extended holiday.

He had vaguely imagined her on a scenic coach tour of Spain to visit places of historical and architectural interest. He knew she liked history. No doubt the majority of the other people on the tour would be pensioners and she would strike up a friendship with a spinster, or perhaps a widow who was travelling alone and who would be grateful for Sara's innately kind nature.

Alekos's rather cosy picture of his PA's holiday plans had been disrupted when she'd told him that she was going away on a YFS trip—which stood for Young, Free and Single. As their name suggested, the tour operator specialised in holidays for people in the twenty-something age bracket who wanted to spend every night clubbing, or partying on a beach. The media often reported scenes of drunken debauchery by Brits in Benidorm. When he had pointed out that a better name for the holiday company would be AFS—Available For Sex—Sara had laughed and, to Alekos's astonishment, told him she was looking forward to letting her hair down in Spain.

His eyes were drawn back to her hair. He visualised her as she had looked every weekday for the past two years. She had always worn her nondescript brown hair scraped back from her face and piled on top of her head in a no-nonsense bun that defied gravity with the aid of an arsenal of metal hairpins.

'You're wearing your hair in a new style,' he said abruptly. 'I was trying to work out why you look different.'

'Mmm, I had it cut while I was away. It was so long, almost waist length, and I was fed up of having to tie it up all the time.' She ran her fingers through the silky layers of her new hairstyle. In the sunshine streaming through the window, her hair seemed to shimmer like gold in places and Alekos felt an unexpected tightening sensation in his groin.

'And I finally ditched my glasses for contact lenses. Although I must admit they're taking a while to get used to.' Sara sounded rueful. 'My new contacts make my eyes water sometimes.'

Alekos was relieved that she wasn't fluttering her eyelashes at him seductively, but she was blinking presumably because her contact lenses felt strange. Without the thick-rimmed glasses he was used to seeing her wearing, her cheekbones were more noticeable and her face was prettier than his memory served him.

He wondered if she'd had some sort of surgical procedure to her lips. Surely he would have remembered the fullness of her lips—and, *Theos,* that faint pout of her lower lip that tempted him to test its softness with his own mouth. He forced his mind away from such a ridiculous idea and reminded himself that this was Miss Mouse, the name that one of his legion of leggy blonde mistresses had unkindly christened Sara.

The nickname had suited her plain looks but not her dry wit that frequently amused Alekos, or her sharp mind and even sharper tongue that he had come to respect, because Sara Lovejoy was the only woman he had ever met who wasn't afraid to state her opinion—even if it was different to his.

'I'll put your coffee on your desk, shall I?' Without waiting for him to reply, Sara walked across the room and placed a cup of coffee on the desk in front of Alekos's chair. He could not help himself from focusing on the sensual undulation of her hips as she walked, and when she leaned across the desk her skirt pulled tighter across the curves of her buttocks.

Alekos cleared his throat audibly and tightened his fingers on the handle of his briefcase as he moved it in front of him to hide the evidence that he was aroused. What the blazes was the matter with him? For the first time in a month he had woken in a good mood this morning, knowing that Sara would be back and between them they would clear the backlog of work that had built up while she'd been away.

But work was the last thing on his mind when she turned to face him and he noticed how her pink silk shirt lovingly moulded the firm swell of her breasts. The top two buttons on her blouse were undone, not enough to reveal any cleavage but more than enough to quicken his pulse as he visualised himself removing her shirt and her lace-edged bra that he could see outlined beneath the silky material of her top.

He forced his gaze away from her breasts down to her surprisingly slim waist and cleared his throat again. 'You...er...appear to have lost some weight.'

'A few pounds, as a matter of fact. I expect it was down to all the exercise I did while I was on holiday.'

What sort of exercise had she done on a young, free and single's holiday? Alekos was not usually prone to flights of imagination but his mind was bombarded with pictures of his new-look PA discarding her inhibitions and enjoying energetic nights with a Spanish Lothario.

'Ah, yes, your holiday. I hope you enjoyed yourself?'

'I certainly did.'

Her grin made him think of a satisfied cat that had drunk a bowlful of cream. 'I'm glad to hear it,' he said tersely. 'But you are not on holiday now, so I'm wondering why you've come to work wearing clothes that are more suitable for the beach than the office.'

When Alekos spoke in that coldly disapproving tone, people tended to immediately take notice and respond with the respect he commanded. But Sara simply shrugged and smoothed her hand over her skirt.

'Oh, I wore a lot less than this on the beach. It's perfectly acceptable for women to go topless on the beaches in the French Riviera.'

Had Sara gone topless? He tried to banish the vision of his prim PA displaying her bare breasts in public. 'I thought you went to Spain for your holiday?'

'I changed my plans at the last minute.'

While Alekos was registering the fact that his ultra-organised PA had apparently changed her holiday destination on a whim, Sara strolled towards him. Why had he never noticed until now that her green eyes sparkled like emeralds when she smiled? He was irritated with himself for thinking such poetic nonsense but he could not stop staring at her.

Along with her new hairstyle and clothes, she was wearing a different perfume: a seductive scent which combined spiky citrus with deeper, exotically floral notes that stirred his senses—and stirred a lot more besides, he acknowledged derisively when he felt himself harden.

'So, where do you want me?' she murmured.

'What?' He stiffened as a picture leapt into his mind of Sara sprawled on the leather sofa with her skirt rucked up around her waist and her legs spread wide, waiting for him to position himself between her thighs.

Cursing beneath his breath, Alekos fought to control his rampant libido and realised that his PA was giving him an odd look. 'Shall I sort out the pile of paperwork on my desk that I presume the temp left for me to deal with, or do you want me to stay in here and take notes from you?' she repeated patiently.

She put her hands on her hips, drawing his attention to the narrowness of her waist that served to emphasise the rounded curves of her breasts. 'I understand that the temp I arranged to cover my absence only lasted a week, and HR organised three more replacements but you dismissed them after a few days.'

'They were all useless,' he snapped. Glancing at his watch, Alekos discovered that he had wasted ten minutes ogling his PA, who normally did not warrant more than a five second glance. He felt unsettled by his awareness of Sara as an attractive woman and was annoyed with himself for his physical response to her. 'I hope you are prepared for the fact that we have a ton of work to catch up on.'

'I guessed you'd have me tied to my desk when I came back to work,' she said airily.

Alekos's eyes narrowed on her serene expression, and he was thrown by the idea that she knew the effect she was having on him. His mental vision of her tied, face down, across her desk made his blood sizzle. He felt confused by his inability to control his response to her.

This was dull, drab Sara—although, admittedly, he had never found her dull when she'd made it clear, soon after he'd promoted her from a secretary in the accounts department to his PA, that she wasn't going to worship him like most women did. But her frumpy appearance had been one reason why he had chosen her. His position as chairman of GE demanded his absolute focus and there was no risk of him being distracted by Miss Mouse.

Alekos had become chairman of the company, which specialised in building luxury superyachts, two years ago, following the death of his father, and he had decided that Sara's unexciting appearance, exemplary secretarial skills and excellent work ethic would make her his ideal PA.

He walked around his desk, lowered his long frame into his chair and took a sip of coffee before he glanced at her. 'I need to make a few phone calls and no doubt you will have plenty of stuff to catch up on, so come back in half an hour and bring the Viceroy file with you.'

'Aren't you forgetting something? The word *please*,' Sara reminded him crisply when he raised his brows questioningly. 'Honestly, Alekos, no wonder you frightened off four temps in as many weeks if you were as surly with them as you're behaving this morning. I suppose you've got woman trouble? That's the usual reason when you come to work with a face like thunder.'

'You must know by now that I never allow my relationships to last long enough for women to become troublesome,' Alekos said smoothly. He leaned back in his chair and gave her a hard stare. 'Remind me again, Sara, why I tolerate your insolence?'

Across the room he saw her eyes sparkle and her mouth curve into a smile that inexplicably made Alekos feel as if he'd been punched in his gut. 'Because I'm good at my job and you don't want to sleep with me. That's what you told me at my interview and I assume nothing has changed?'

She stepped out of his office and closed the door behind her before he could think of a suitably cutting retort. He glared at the space where she had been standing seconds earlier. *Theos*, sometimes she overstepped the mark. His nostrils flared with annoyance. He could not explain the odd sensation in the pit of his stomach when he caught the drift of her perfume that still lingered in the room.

He felt rattled by Sara's startling physical transformation from frump to sexpot. But he reminded himself that her honesty was one of the things he admired about her. He doubted that any of the three hundred employees at Gionakis Enterprises' London offices, and probably none of the three thousand staff employed by the company worldwide, would dream of speaking to him as bluntly as Sara did. It made a refreshing change to have someone challenge him when most people, especially women, always said yes to him.

He briefly wondered what she would say if he told her that he had changed his mind and wanted to take her to bed. Would she be willing to have sex with him, or would Sara be the only woman to refuse him? Alekos was almost tempted to find out. But practicality outweighed his inconvenient and, he confidently assumed, fleeting attraction to her, when he reminded himself that there were any number of women who would be happy to help him relieve his sexual frustration but a good PA was worth her weight in gold.

The day's schedule was packed. Alekos opened his laptop but, unusually for him, he could not summon any enthusiasm for work. He swivelled his chair round to the window and stared down at the busy street five floors below, where red London buses, black taxis and kamikaze cyclists competed for road space.

He liked living in England's capital city, although he much preferred the current June sunshine to the dank drizzle and short days of the winter. After his father's death it had been expected by the members of the board, and his family, that Alekos would move back to Greece permanently and run the company from GE's offices in Athens. His father, Kostas Gionakis, and before him Alekos's grandfather, the founder of the company, had both done so.

His decision to move the company's headquarters to London had been mainly for business reasons. London was closer to GE's growing client list in Florida and the Bahamas, and the cosmopolitan capital was ideally suited to entertain a clientele made up exclusively of millionaires and billionaires, who were prepared to spend eye-watering amounts of cash on a superyacht—the ultimate status symbol.

On a personal front, Alekos had been determined to establish himself as the new company chairman away from his father's power base in Greece. The grand building in Athens which had been GE's headquarters looked like a palace and Kostas Gionakis had been king. Alekos never forgot that he was the usurper to the throne.

His jaw clenched. Dimitri should have been chairman, not him. But his brother was dead—killed twenty years ago, supposedly in a tragic accident. Alekos's parents had been devastated and he had never told them of his suspicions about the nature of Dimitri's death.

Alekos had been fourteen at the time, the youngest in the family, born six years after Dimitri and after their three sisters. He had idolised his brother. Everyone had admired the Gionakis heir. Dimitri was handsome, athletic and clever and had been groomed from boyhood to take over running the family business. Alekos was the spare heir should the unthinkable happen to Dimitri.

But the unthinkable *had* happened. Dimitri had died and Alekos had suddenly become the future of the company—a fact that his father had never allowed him to forget.

Had Kostas believed that his youngest son would make as good a chairman of GE as his firstborn son?

Alekos doubted it. He had felt that he was second best in his father's eyes. He knew that was still the opinion of some of the board members who disapproved of his playboy lifestyle.

But he would prove those who doubted his abilities wrong. In the two years that he had been chairman the company's profits had increased and they were expanding into new markets around the globe. Perhaps his father would have been proud of him. Alekos would never know. But what he knew for sure was that he could not allow himself to be distracted by his PA simply because her sexy new look had stirred his desire.

Turning away from the window, he opened a document on his laptop and resolutely focused on work. He had inherited the company by default. He owed it to Dimitri's memory to ensure that Gionakis Enterprises continued to be as successful as it had been when his father was chairman, and as Alekos was sure it would have been under his brother's leadership.

Sara ignored a stab of guilt as she passed her desk, piled with paperwork that required her attention, and hurried into the bathroom. The mirror above the sink confirmed her fears. Her flushed cheeks and dilated pupils betrayed her reaction to Alekos that she had been unable to control.

She felt as though she had been holding her breath the entire time she had been in his office. Why was it that she'd managed to hide her awareness of him for two years but when she had set eyes on him this morning after she hadn't seen him for a month her pulse-rate had rocketed and her mouth had felt dry?

The sensation of her heart slamming against her ribcage whenever she was in close proximity to Alekos wasn't new, but she had perfected the art of hiding her emotions behind a cool smile, aware that her job depended on it. When Alekos had elevated her to the role of his PA over several other suitably qualified candidates for the job, he had bluntly told her that he never mixed business with pleasure and there was no chance of a sexual relationship developing between them. His arrogance had irritated Sara and she'd almost told him that she had no intention of copying her mother's mistake by having an affair with her boss.

During the eighteen months that she had worked in the accounts department before her promotion, she'd heard that the company's board members disapproved of Alekos's playboy lifestyle, which attracted the wrong type of press interest, and she understood why he was determined to keep his relationship with his staff on a strictly professional footing. What Alekos wanted from his PA was efficiency, dedication and the ability to blend into the background—and plain, conservatively dressed Sara had fitted the bill perfectly.

In truth she would have worn a nun's habit to the office if Alekos had required her to because she was so keen to secure the job. Her promotion to personal assistant of the chairman of Gionakis Enterprises had finally won her mother's praise. For the first time in her life she had felt that she wasn't a disappointment to Joan Lovejoy. The surname was a misnomer if ever there was one because, as far as Sara could tell, there had been no love or joy in her mother's life.

She'd wondered if her mother had loved the man who'd abandoned her after he had made her pregnant. But Joan had refused to reveal Sara's father's identity and only ever made a few oblique references to him, notably that he had once been an Oxford don and it was a pity that Sara hadn't inherited his academic brilliance.

Sara had spent most of her life comparing herself to a nameless, faceless man who had helped to create her but she had never met—until six weeks ago. Now she knew that she had inherited her green eyes from her father. He was no longer faceless, or nameless. His name was Lionel Kingsley and he was a well-known politician. She'd been stunned when he had phoned her and revealed that there was a possibility she might be his daughter. She had agreed to a DNA test to see if he was really her father but she had been sure of the result before the test had proved it. When she looked into a mirror she saw her father's eyes looking back at her.

For the first time in her life she felt she was a whole person, and so many things about herself suddenly made sense, like her love of art and her creativity that she'd always suppressed because her mother had pushed her to concentrate on academic subjects.

Lionel was a widower and had two grown-up children. Her half-siblings! Sara felt excited and nervous at the thought of meeting her half-brother and half-sister. She understood Lionel's concern that his son and daughter from his marriage might be upset to learn that he had an illegitimate daughter, and she had told herself to be patient and wait until he was ready to acknowledge publicly that he was her father. Finally it was going to happen. Lionel had invited her to his home at the weekend so that he could introduce her to Freddie and Charlotte Kingsley.

Sara had seen pictures of them and discovered that she bore a striking resemblance to her half-siblings. But the physical similarities between her and her half-sister did not apply to their very different dress styles. Photographs of Charlotte wearing stylish, figure-hugging clothes had made Sara realise how frumpy she looked in comparison. The smart suits she wore to the office reflected the importance of her role as PA to the chairman of the company and she had reminded herself that if Alekos had wanted a decorative bimbo to be his PA he wouldn't have chosen her.

The new clothes she had bought while she had been on holiday did not make her look like a bimbo, Sara reassured herself. The skirt and blouse she was wearing were perfectly respectable for the office. Shopping in the chic boutiques on the French Riviera where her father owned a holiday villa had been a revelation. Remembering the photos she'd seen of her stylish half-sister had prompted Sara to try on colourful summery outfits. She had dropped a dress size from plenty of swimming and playing tennis and she loved being able to fit into skirts and dresses that showed off her more toned figure.

She ran her fingers through her new layered hairstyle. She still wasn't used to her hair swishing around her shoulders when she turned her head. It made her feel more feminine and, well...*sexy*. She'd had a few blonde highlights put through the front sections of her hair to complement the natural lighter streaks from where she had spent a month in the French sunshine.

Maybe it was true that blondes *did* have more fun. But the truth was that meeting her father had given her a new sense of self-confidence. The part of her that had been missing was now complete, and Sara didn't want to fade into the background any more. Travelling to work on the Tube this morning, she'd wondered if Alekos would notice her changed appearance.

She stared at her flushed face in the mirror and grimaced. All right, she had *hoped* he would notice her, instead of treating her like a piece of office furniture: functional, necessary but utterly uninteresting.

Well, she had got her wish. Alekos had stopped dead in his tracks when he'd seen her and his shocked expression had changed to a speculative gleam as his eyes had roamed over her. Heat had swept through her body when his gaze lingered on her breasts. She felt embarrassed thinking he might have noticed that her nipples had hardened in a telltale sign that he excited her more than any man had ever done.

Her decision to revamp her appearance suddenly seemed like a bad idea. When she'd dressed in dowdy clothes she hadn't had to worry that Alekos might catch her glancing at him a dozen times a day, because he rarely seemed to notice that she was a human being and not a robot. Remembering the hot, hard gleam in his eyes when she had been in his office just now sent a tremor through her, and a little part of her wished she could rush back home and change into her safe navy blue suit. But when she'd returned home from her holiday she'd found that all her old clothes were too big, and she'd packed them into black sacks and donated them to a charity shop.

There was no going back. The old Sara Lovejoy was gone for ever and the new Sara was here to stay. Alekos would just have to get used to it.

CHAPTER TWO

AT EXACTLY NINE THIRTY, Sara knocked on Alekos's door and took a deep breath before she stepped into his office. He was sitting behind his desk, leaning back in his chair that was half turned towards the window, and he was holding his phone to his ear. He spared her a brief glance and then swung his gaze back to the window while he continued his telephone conversation.

She ordered herself not to feel disappointed by his lack of interest. Obviously she must have imagined that earlier he had looked at her with a glint of desire in his eyes. Just because she had a new hairstyle and clothes did not mean that she had become Alekos's fantasy woman. She knew his type: elegant blondes with legs that went on for ever. In the past two years a steady stream of models and socialites had arrived in his life and exited it a few months later when Alekos had grown bored of his affair with them.

Sara had hoped she would be able to control her reaction to Alekos but her heart leapt wildly in her chest as she studied his profile. Slashing cheekbones, a square jaw shadowed with dark stubble and eyes that gleamed like polished jet all combined to give him a lethal magnetism that women invariably found irresistible. His thick black hair had a habit of falling forwards across his brow and she was tempted to run her fingers through it. As for his mouth... Her eyes were drawn to his beautiful mouth. Full-lipped and sensual when he was relaxed and utterly devastating when he smiled, his mouth could also curve into a cynical expression when he wished to convey his displeasure.

'Don't stand there wasting time, Sara.' Alekos's voice made her jump, and she flushed as she registered that he had finished his phone call and had caught her out staring at him. 'We have a lot to get through.'

'I was waiting for you to finish your call.' She was thankful that two years of practice at hiding her reaction to his smouldering sensuality allowed her to sound calm and composed even though her heart was racing. The way he growled her name in his sexy accent, drawing out the second syllable... Sara*aaa*...was curiously intimate—as if they were lovers. But of course they were not lovers and were never likely to be.

She forced herself to walk unhurriedly across the room, but with every step that took her closer to Alekos's desk she was conscious of his unswerving gaze. The unholy gleam in his eyes made her feel as if he were mentally undressing her. Every centimetre of her skin was on fire when she sat down on the chair in front of his desk.

It would be easy to be overwhelmed by him. But when she had been promoted to his PA she'd realised that Alekos was surrounded by people who always agreed with him, and she had decided that she could not allow herself to be intimidated by his powerful personality. She'd noted that he did not have much respect for the flunkeys and hangers-on who were so anxious to keep on the right side of him.

She had very quickly proved that she was good at her job, but the first time she had disagreed with Alekos over a work issue he'd clearly been astounded to discover that his mousy assistant had a backbone. After a tense stand-off, when Sara had refused to back down, he had narrowed his gaze on her determined expression and something like admiration had flickered in his dark eyes.

She valued his respect more than anything because she loved her job. Working for Alekos was like riding a roller coaster at a theme park: exciting, intense and fast-paced, and it was the knowledge that she would never find a job as rewarding as her current one that made Sara take a steadying breath. She could not deny it was flattering that Alekos had finally noticed her, but if she wanted to continue in her role as his PA she must ignore the predatory glint in his eyes.

She held her pencil poised over her notepad and gave him a cool smile. 'I'm ready to start when you are.'

Her breezy tone seemed to irritate him. 'I doubt you'll be so cheerful by the time we've finished today. I'll need you to work late this evening.'

'Sorry, but I can't stay late tonight. I've made other plans.'

He frowned. 'Well, change them. Do I need to remind you that a requirement of your job is for you to work whatever hours I dictate, within reason?'

'I'm sure I don't need to remind you that I have always worked extra when you've asked me to,' Sara said calmly. 'And I've worked *unreasonable* hours, such as when we stayed up until one a.m. to put together a sales pitch for a sheikh before he flew back to Dubai. It paid off too, because Sheikh Al Mansoor placed an order for a one-hundred-million-pound yacht from GE.'

Alekos's scowl did not make him any less gorgeous; in fact it gave him a dangerous, brooding look that turned Sara's bones to liquid.

'I can stay late every other night this week if you need me to,' she went on in an effort to appease him. Alekos's bad mood threatened to spoil her excitement about meeting her father after work. Lionel Kingsley's high profile as an MP meant that he did not want to risk being seen in public with Sara. As they couldn't go to a restaurant, she had invited him to her home and was planning to cook dinner for him before he attended an evening engagement.

'Oh, I can't stay late on Friday either,' she said. 'And actually I'd like to leave an hour early because I'm going away for the weekend.' She remembered the plans she'd made to visit her father at his house in Berkshire. 'I'll work through my lunch hour to make up the time.'

'Well, well.' Alekos's sardonic drawl put Sara on her guard. 'You go away for a month and return sporting a new haircut, a new—and much improved, I have to say—wardrobe, and now suddenly you have a busy social life. It makes me wonder if a man is the reason for the new-look Sara Lovejoy.'

'My personal life is none of your business,' she said composedly. Technically, she supposed that a man was the reason for the change in her, but she had not met a lover, as Alekos had implied. She had enjoyed getting to know her father when he had invited her to spend her holiday at his villa in the south of France but she had promised Lionel that she wouldn't tell anyone she was his daughter.

Deep down she felt disappointed that her father wished to keep their relationship secret. It was as if Lionel was ashamed of her. But she reminded herself that he had promised to introduce her to her half-siblings on Friday, and perhaps then he would openly welcome her as his daughter. She pulled her mind back to the present when she realised Alekos was speaking.

'It will be my business if your work is affected because you're mooning over some guy.'

Sara still refused to rise to Alekos's verbal baiting. She tapped the tip of her pencil on her pad and said with heavy emphasis, '*I'm* ready to start work when you are.'

Alekos picked up a client's folder from the pile on his desk, but he did not open it. Instead he leaned back in his chair, an unreadable expression on his handsome face as he surveyed her for long minutes while her tension grew and she was sure he must see the pulse beating erratically at the base of her throat.

'Why did you change your holiday plans and go to France rather than Spain?'

'The holiday company I'd booked with cancelled my trip, but a…friend invited me to stay at his villa in Antibes.'

'Would this friend be the man whose voice I heard in the background when I phoned you with a query from the Miami office a week ago?'

Sara tensed. Could Alekos possibly have recognised her famous father's voice?

'Why are you suddenly fascinated with my private life?'

'I'm merely concerned for your well-being and offering a timely reminder that holiday romances notoriously don't last.'

'For goodness' sake!' Sara told herself not to be fooled by Alekos's 'concern for her wellbeing'. His real concern was he did not want his PA moping about or unable to concentrate on her work because she'd suffered a broken heart. 'What makes you think I had a holiday romance?'

He trailed his eyes over her, subjecting her to a thorough appraisal that brought a flush to her cheeks. 'It's obvious. Before you went on holiday you wore frumpy clothes that camouflaged your figure. But after spending a month in France you have undergone a transformation into a frankly very attractive young woman. It docsn't take a detective to work out that a love affair is probably the cause of your new-found sensuality.'

'Well, of course *you* would assume that a *man* is the reason I've altered my appearance.' Sara's temper simmered. 'It couldn't be that I decided to update my wardrobe for *me*.' His cynical expression fuelled her anger but she also felt hurt. Had she really looked so awful in her navy blue suit with her hair secured in a neat bun, as Alekos had said? It was pathetic the way her heart had leapt when he'd complimented her new look and told her she was attractive.

'You are such a male chauvinist,' she snapped. Ignoring the warning glint in his eyes, she said furiously, 'I suppose you think I altered the way I dress in the hope of impressing you?'

The landline phone on his desk rang and Sara instinctively reached out to answer it. Simultaneously Alekos did the same and, as his fingers brushed against hers, she felt a sizzle of electricity shoot up her arm.

'Oh!' She tried to snatch her hand away, but he snaked his fingers around her wrist and stroked his thumb pad over her thudding pulse.

'When you dressed to come to work this morning, did you choose your outfit to please me?' His black eyes burned like hot coals into hers.

Sara flushed guiltily. 'Of course not.' She refused to admit to herself, let alone to Alekos, that for the past two years she had fantasised about him desiring her. She stared at his chiselled face and swallowed. 'Are you going to answer the call?' she said breathlessly.

To her relief, he let go of her wrist and picked up the phone. She resisted the urge to leap out of her seat and run out of his office. Instead she made herself stroll across the room to the coffee machine. The familiar routine of pouring water into the machine's reservoir and inserting a coffee capsule into the compartment gave her a few moments' breathing space to bring herself under control.

Why had she goaded Alekos like that? She had always been careful to hide her attraction to him but he must have noticed how the pulse in her wrist had almost jumped through her skin because it had been beating so hard, echoing the thudding beat of her heart.

She could not put off carrying their coffees over to his desk any longer, and she was thankful that Alekos did not glance at her when he finished his phone call and opened the file in front of him. He waited for her to sit down and pick up her notepad before he began to dictate at breakneck speed, making no allowances for the fact that she hadn't taken shorthand notes for a month.

It set the tone for the rest of the day as they worked

together to clear the backlog that had built up while Sara had been away. At five o'clock she rolled her aching shoulders and went to the bathroom to brush her hair and apply a fresh coat of rose-pink lip gloss that was her new must-have item of make-up.

In Alekos's office she found him standing by his desk. He was massaging the back of his neck as if he felt as tired from their busy day as she was. She had forgotten how tall he was. He had inherited his six-foot-four height from his maternal grandfather, who had been a Canadian, he'd once explained to Sara. But in every other aspect he was typically Greek, from his dark olive complexion and mass of black hair to his arrogant belief that he only had to click his fingers and women would flock to him. The trouble was that they did, Sara thought ruefully.

Alekos was used to having any woman he wanted. She told herself it was lucky that there had been no repeat of the breathless moments that had occurred earlier in the day, when rampant desire had blazed in his eyes as he'd trapped her wrist and felt the giveaway throb of her sexual awareness of him.

He must have heard his office door open, and turned his head in her direction. They had played out the same scene hundreds of times before, and most days when she came to check if he needed her to do anything else before she went home he did not bother looking up from his computer screen as he bid her goodnight. But he was looking at her now. She watched his hard features tauten and become almost wolf-like as he stared at her with a hungry gleam in his eyes that excited her and filled her with illicit longing.

Something tugged in the pit of her stomach, tugged

hard like a knot being pulled tighter and tighter, as if an invisible thread linked her body to Alekos. And then he blinked and the feral glitter in his eyes disappeared. Perhaps it had never been there and she had imagined that he'd stared at her as if he wanted to devour her?

'I'm just off now.' She was amazed that her voice sounded normal when her insides were in turmoil. 'I'll finish typing up the report for the shareholders first thing tomorrow.'

'Did you remember that we are attending the annual dinner for the board members on Thursday evening?'

She nodded. 'I'll bring the dress I'm going to wear for the dinner to work and get changed here at the office like I did for the Christmas party.'

'You had better check with the restaurant that they won't be serving seafood. Orestis Pagnotis is allergic to it and, much as I'd like to have the old man off my back, I'd better not allow him to risk suffering a possibly fatal reaction,' Alekos said drily.

'I've already given the restaurant a list of the dietary requirements of the guests.' She smiled sympathetically. 'Is Orestis still being a problem?'

He shrugged. 'He's one of the old school. He joined the board when my grandfather was chairman, and he was a close friend of my father.' Alekos gave a frustrated sigh. 'Orestis believes I take too many risks and he has the support of some of the other board members, who fail to understand that the company needs to move with the times rather than remain in the Stone Age. Orestis's latest gripe is that he thinks the chairman should be married.'

Alekos muttered something in Greek that Sara guessed was not complimentary about the influential board member. 'According to Orestis, if I take a wife it will prove that I have left my playboy days behind and I will be more focused on running GE.'

Her heart dipped. 'Are you considering getting married?'

Somehow she managed to inject the right amount of casual interest into her voice. She knew he had ended his affair with a stunning Swedish model called Danika shortly before her holiday, but in the month she had been away it was likely that he had met someone else. Alekos never stayed celibate for long.

Perhaps he had fallen in love with the woman of his dreams. It was possible that Alekos might ask her to organise his wedding. She would have to pin a smile on her face and hide her heartache while she made arrangements for him and his beautiful bride—she was certain to be beautiful—to spend their honeymoon at an exotic location. Sara pulled her mind away from her unwelcome thoughts when she realised Alekos was speaking.

'I'll have to marry eventually.' He sounded unenthusiastic at the prospect. 'I am the last male Gionakis and my mother and sisters remind me at every opportunity that it is my duty to produce an heir. Obviously I will first have to select a suitable wife.'

'How do you intend to *select a suitable wife*?' She could not hide her shock that he had such a cavalier attitude towards marriage. 'Will you hold interviews and ask the candidates, who are your potential brides, to fill out a detailed questionnaire about themselves?' She was aware that her voice had risen and Alekos's amused smile infuriated her further.

'Your suggestion is not a bad idea. Why are you so outraged?' he said smoothly.

'Because you make marriage sound like a…a cattle market where finding a wife is like choosing a prize heifer to breed from. What about love?'

'What about it?' He studied her flushed face speculatively. 'Statistically, somewhere between forty and fifty per cent of marriages end in divorce, and I bet that most of those marriages were so-called love matches. But with such a high failure rate it seems sensible to take emotion out of the equation and base marriage on social and financial compatibility, mutual respect and the pursuit of shared goals such as bringing up a family.'

Sara shook her head. 'Your arrogance is unbelievable. You accuse some of GE's board members of being stuck in the Stone Age, but your views on marriage are Neolithic. Women nowadays don't sit around twiddling their thumbs and hoping that a rich man will choose them to be his wife.'

'You'd be surprised,' Alekos murmured drily. 'When I decide to marry—in another ten years or so—I don't envisage I'll have a problem finding a woman who is willing to marry a multimillionaire.'

'Well, I wouldn't marry for money,' Sara said fiercely. Deep inside her she felt an ache of regret that Alekos had trampled on her silly dream that he would one day fall in love with her. Realistically, she knew it would never happen but hearing him state so emphatically that he did not aspire to a marriage built on love forced her to accept that she must get over her embarrassing crush on him.

'You would prefer to gamble your future happiness on a fickle emotion that poets try to convince us is love? But of course love is simply a sanitized word for lust.'

'If you're asking me whether I believe in love, then

the answer is yes, I do. Why are you so sceptical, Alekos? You once told me that your parents had been happily married for forty-five years before your father died.'

'And therein proves my point. My parents had an arranged marriage which was extremely successful. Love wasn't necessary, although I believe they grew to be very fond of each other over the course of their marriage.'

Sara gave up. 'You're just a cynic.'

'No, I'm a realist. There is a dark side to love and I have witnessed its destructive power.'

A memory slid into Alekos's mind of that fateful day twenty years ago when he'd found Dimitri walking along the beach. His brother's eyes had been red-rimmed and he'd wept as he'd told Alekos he had discovered that his girlfriend had been unfaithful. It was the last time Alekos had seen Dimitri alive.

'Love is an illusion,' he told Sara harshly, 'and you would do well to remember it before you rush to give away your heart to a man you only met a few weeks ago.'

After Sara had gone, Alekos walked over to the window and a few minutes later he saw her emerge from the GE building and walk along the pavement. Even from a distance he noted the sexy wiggle of her hips when she walked and a shaft of white-hot lust ripped through him.

He swore. Lusting after his PA was so unexpected and he assured himself that his reaction to Sara's transformation from dowdy to a very desirable woman was down to sexual frustration. He hadn't had sex since he'd split from his last mistress almost two months ago.

'What are you looking for?' Danika had asked him when he'd told her their affair was over. 'You say you don't want permanence in a relationship, but what do you want?'

Right now he wanted a woman under him, Alekos thought, conscious of his erection pressing uncomfortably against the zip of his trousers. A memory flashed into his mind of Sara leaning across his desk with her skirt pulled tight over her bottom. He imagined her without her skirt, her derrière presented for him to slide her panties down so that he could stroke his hands over her naked body. In his fantasy he had already removed her blouse and bra and he stood behind her and slid his arms round her to cup her firm breasts in his hands...

Theos! Alekos raked his hand through his hair and forced his mind away from his erotic thoughts. Sara was the best PA he'd ever had and he was determined not to damage their excellent working relationship. She was the only woman, apart from his mother and sisters, who he trusted. She was discreet, loyal and she made his life easier in countless ways that he had not fully appreciated until she had taken a month's holiday.

If he made her his mistress he would not be able to continue to employ her as his PA. Office affairs did not work, especially after the affair ended—and of course it would end after a few months at most. He had a low boredom threshold and there was no reason to think that his surprising attraction to Sara would last long once he'd taken her to bed.

Alekos turned his thoughts to the party he was due to attend that evening. Perhaps he would meet a woman who would hold his attention for more than an hour. He received many more invitations to social functions than he had the time or the inclination to attend, but he had a particular reason for accepting an invitation to a party being given by a wealthy city banker. Alekos knew that a Texan oil baron would be included on the guest list. Warren McCuskey was looking to buy a superyacht to keep his wife, who was twenty years younger than him, happy, and Alekos was determined to persuade the billionaire Texan to buy a yacht from GE.

From his vantage point at the window he continued to watch Sara standing in the street below. She seemed to be waiting for someone. A large black saloon car drew up alongside her, the rear door opened and she climbed into the car before it pulled away from the kerb.

He was intrigued. Why hadn't Sara's 'friend' got out of the car to greet her? Earlier, she had been oddly secretive about her boyfriend. And what was the real reason for her attractive new look? Alekos couldn't remember the last time a woman had aroused his curiosity and it was ironic that the woman who had fired his interest had been under his nose for the past two years.

CHAPTER THREE

ON THURSDAY EVENING, Alekos checked the gold watch on his wrist and frowned when he saw that he and Sara needed to leave for the board members' dinner in the next five minutes. Usually when she accompanied him to work functions she was ready in plenty of time. He was annoyed that she had not been waiting for him when he'd walked out of the private bathroom next to his office, where he had showered and changed.

He wondered what she would wear to the dinner. He remembered that a few months ago it had been a particularly busy time at work and Sara had stayed at the office until late, only dashing off to change for the staff Christmas party ten minutes before it was due to start. She had emerged from the cloakroom wearing what he had supposed was a ball gown, but the long black dress had resembled a shroud and had the effect of draining all the colour from her face.

He had been tempted to order her to go and buy something more cheerful. The shop windows were full of mannequins displaying party dresses for the festive season. But then he'd remembered that Sara was grieving for her mother, who had recently died. For once he had studied her closely, and her pinched face and

the shadows beneath her eyes had evoked a faint tug
of sympathy for his PA, who reminded him of a drab
sparrow.

Alekos turned his thoughts to the present. The board
members' dinner was a prestigious event that called
for him to wear a tuxedo, but he refused to be clean
shaven. He glanced in the mirror and grimaced as he
ran his hand over the trimmed black stubble on his jaw.
No doubt his nemesis Orestis Pagnotis would accuse
him of looking more like a pirate than the chairman of
a billion-pound company.

Behind him the office door opened and Sara stepped
into the room. His jaw dropped as he stared at her reflection in the mirror, and he was thankful he had his
back to her so that she couldn't see the betraying bulge
of his erection beneath his trousers.

The drab sparrow had metamorphosed into a pea-
cock. Somewhere in Alekos's stunned brain he registered that the description was all the more apt because
her dress was peacock-blue silk and the long skirt gave
an iridescent shimmer when she walked. The top of
the dress was high-necked and sleeveless, leaving her
shoulders bare. A sparkling diamanté belt showed off
her slender waist.

From the front, the dress was elegant and Alekos
had no problem with it. But when Sara turned around
to check that the espresso machine was switched off, he
saw that her dress was backless to the base of her spine.
A hot haze of desire made his blood pound through
his veins.

'You can't wear that,' he rasped, shock and lust stran-
gling his vocal cords. 'Half the board members are over
sixty and I know for a fact that a couple of them have

weak hearts. If they see you in that dress they're likely
to suffer a cardiac arrest.'

She looked genuinely confused. 'What's wrong with
my dress?'

'Half of it is missing.'

'Well, technically I suppose that's true. But I don't
suppose the sight of my shoulder blades will evoke wild
lust in anyone.'

Don't bet on it, Alekos thought grimly. He would
not have believed that a woman's bare back could be
so erotic. The expanse of Sara's skin revealed by the
backless dress invited him to trace his fingertips down
her spine and then spread his hand over her tempting
nakedness.

Theos, what he actually wanted to do was stride over
to her, sweep her into his arms and ravish her thoroughly and to their mutual satisfaction on top of his
desk. That particular fantasy had been a common theme
for the past four days, which had frankly been tortur-
ous. Sara had turned up for work each morning wearing outfits that had sent his blood pressure soaring. Her
stylish skirts and blouses had hugged her curvy figure
without being too revealing, and somehow the hint of
her sexy figure beneath her clothes was much more exciting than if she had worn a miniskirt and boob tube.

He checked the time again and realised they would
have to leave immediately or risk being late for the dinner. 'God knows what the board members will make of
you dressed like a glamour model in a men-only mag-
azine,' he growled as he held the door open and then
followed Sara into the corridor. 'You know how con-
servative some of them are.' He shoved his hands into
his pockets out of harm's way, but he could not control

the hard thud of his heart, or the hard throb of another part of his anatomy, he acknowledged derisively.

'Nonsense, they'll think I'm wearing a perfectly nice dress,' she said serenely. 'The board members like me. They know I work hard and I would never do anything that might harm the company's image.'

Alekos had to admit she was right. Even his main critic Orestis Pagnotis approved of Sara and had remarked to Alekos that he should consider marrying someone as sensible and down-to-earth as his PA.

The trouble was that Sara no longer looked like his sensible PA. She looked gorgeous and unbelievably sexy, and while Alekos certainly had no thoughts of marrying her he couldn't deny that he wanted her—badly. He was not used to denying himself. But the rules he had made about not getting personally involved with any member of his staff meant that she was forbidden. To a born rebel like himself the word *forbidden* acted like a red rag to a bull. It was a fact of life that you wanted most what you couldn't have, Alekos brooded when they were in the car on the way to the dinner. It was also true that rules were made to be broken.

The restaurant was at a five-star hotel on Park Lane and a private dining room had been booked for the board members' dinner.

'Alekos!' A high-pitched voice assaulted Alekos's ears as he walked into the private function suite, and he swore silently when a young woman ran over to him and greeted him enthusiastically by kissing him on both his cheeks.

'Zelda,' he murmured as he politely but firmly unwound her arms from around his neck. Orestis Pagnotis's granddaughter was as exuberant as a young child but there was nothing childlike about the eighteen-year-old's physical attributes. Alekos was surprised that Orestis had allowed his granddaughter to wear a gold clingy dress with a plunging neckline. But he knew that Zelda was her grandfather's favourite grandchild—a fact she used shamelessly to get her own way.

Zelda had developed a crush on Alekos the previous year when he had spent a few days meeting with some of GE's senior board members aboard the company's flagship yacht, *Artemis*. One night, Alekos had found the teenager waiting for him in his bed. He had managed to persuade her to return to her own cabin and had done his best to avoid her since then.

But the gods were ganging up against him tonight, he decided as Zelda linked her arm possessively though his and he had no choice but to escort her into the salon, where champagne cocktails and canapés were being served. He looked around for Sara and his temper did not improve when he saw her chatting with the new whiz-kid CFO. Paul Eddis was in his early thirties, and Alekos supposed that women might consider his blond hair and rather delicate facial features attractive. Sara certainly looked happy in his company, and Eddis was staring at her with a stunned expression on his face as if he couldn't believe his luck that the most beautiful woman in the room was giving him all her attention.

The evening went from bad to worse when they were called to take their places for dinner and Alekos discovered he was seated next to Zelda. Sara had arranged the seating plan and he'd specifically asked her to put him on a different table from Zelda. Had Sara decided to have a joke at his expense? Alekos glared across the room to where she was sitting at another table. But she was facing away from him and white-hot fury swept through him when he noticed the waiter ogling her bare back.

He forced himself to eat a little of his cheese soufflé, which was as light as air but tasted like cardboard in his mouth. 'Shouldn't you be at school, studying for exams?' he muttered to Zelda as he firmly removed her hand from his thigh.

'I've left school.' She giggled. 'Well, the headmistress insisted I leave because she said I was a bad influence on the other girls. But I don't need to pass exams because I'm going to be a model. Pappoús is paying for me to have my portfolio done with a top photographer.'

'If you don't behave yourself, perhaps your grandfather will refuse to fund your modelling career.'

'Oh, Pappoús will give me anything I ask for.' Zelda leaned closer to Alekos. 'If I don't behave, will you punish me?' she said artfully.

He would like to punish his PA for putting him through an uncomfortable evening. Alekos's furious black gaze bored into Sara's shoulder blades. And yes, they could send a man wild with desire, he discovered. The hellish meal ended eventually but as the band started up and he strode away from the table—ignoring Zelda's plea to dance with her—he was waylaid by Orestis Pagnotis.

The older man glared at Alekos with his gimlet gaze. 'Keep away from my granddaughter. Zelda is an innocent young woman and I will not allow you to corrupt her, Alekos. I've always been concerned that your womanising ways would bring the company into disrepute. I'm sure I don't need to remind you that you need the support of *every* member of the board to implement the changes you want to make within GE.'

Alekos struggled to keep his temper under control. 'Are you threatening me?'

'I suggest you think hard about what I've said,' Orestis warned.

Sara stood up as Alekos approached her table. 'What's wrong? You don't look like you're enjoying the party.'

'I wonder why that is?' he snapped. 'Do you think it could be because you placed me next to Zelda Pagnotis at dinner, after I'd expressly asked you to seat her away from me? Or perhaps it's because Orestis believes that I have designs on his granddaughter, who he thinks is as innocent as a lamb, incidentally.'

'I didn't seat you next to her.' Sara looked puzzled. 'When we arrived I even popped into the dining room to check that the seating plan had been set out as I had organised it… Zelda must have switched the name cards around.'

Alekos's frustration with Orestis's manipulative granddaughter, and his anger with Orestis for threatening to withhold his support at the next board meeting, turned to a different kind of frustration as he stared into Sara's guileless green eyes. Across the room he saw Zelda heading purposefully in his direction. He caught hold of Sara's hand.

'Dance with me,' he ordered, pulling her towards him. She gave him a startled look, but Alekos was too stunned by the fire that ignited inside him when he felt her breasts pressed against his chest to care.

It was impossible to believe that this was the same Sara who had held herself stiffly and ensured that no part of her body touched his when he'd felt duty-bound to ask her to dance with him at the Christmas party. This Sara was soft and pliant in his arms and he was conscious of the hard points of her nipples through his shirt and the surprising firmness of her thighs beneath her silk dress as she moved with him in time to the music.

'I noted that you made sure you were sitting next to Paul Eddis at dinner,' he bit out. The memory of watching Sara leaning her head towards the CFO when they had sat together for the meal evoked an acidic sensation in his gut. *Theos*, was it *jealousy* that had made him want to walk over to Eddis and drag the guy out of his seat? Alekos had never been possessive of a woman in his life, but he felt a burning urge to drape his jacket around Sara's shoulders and hide her naked back from view. 'You are meant to be on duty this evening, not flirting with other members of GE staff, or the waiters.'

Twin spots of colour stained her cheeks and he could tell she was fighting to control her temper. The thought excited Alekos more than it should. He wanted to disturb her composure like she disturbed him.

'I haven't flirted with anyone. You're being ridiculous.'

'Am I?' Alekos succumbed to the demon called temptation and slid his hand up from her waist to her spine. The bare skin of her back was as smooth as silk but, unlike cool silk, her skin was warm and as he spread his fingers wide he felt the heat of her body scald him. 'You must be aware that every man in this room desires you,' he taunted her.

Her eyes widened and he thought he might drown in those mysterious deep green pools. 'Even you?' she taunted him right back.

Her refusal to be cowed by him had earned Alekos's

respect when she'd been his prim, plain secretary. But now her sassy tongue shattered the last vestiges of his restraint.

'What do you think?' he growled as he pressed his hand into the small of her back so that her pelvis came into contact with his. The hard ridge of his arousal could leave her in no doubt of the effect she had on him.

'Alekos…' Sara licked her dry lips. Her intention had been to remind him that they were on the dance floor in full view of GE's board members and senior executives. But, instead of sounding crisply efficient in her best PA manner, her voice emerged as a breathy whisper as if she were starring in a soft porn movie, she thought disgustedly.

'Sara,' he mocked, mimicking her husky tone. The way he said her name in his sexy accent, curling his tongue around each syllable, made her toes curl. When she had danced with him at the Christmas party she'd been so tense, terrified he would guess he was all of her fantasies rolled into one. But he'd caught her off guard when he'd pulled her into his arms just now. Dancing with him, her breasts crushed against his broad chest and her cheek resting on the lapel of his jacket, was divine. Beneath her palm she could feel the hard thud of his heart and recognised that its erratic beat echoed her own.

Every day at the office for the past four days had been a refined torture as she'd struggled to hide her awareness of him. It had been easier when he hadn't noticed her, but since she had returned to work after her holiday she'd been conscious of a simmering sexual chemistry between her and Alekos that she had tried to ignore. To be fair, he had seemed as if he was trying to ignore it too and a lot of the time they had been so stiff and polite with each other, as if they were strangers rather than two people who had built up a comfortable working relationship over two years.

But sometimes when she'd stolen a glance at Alekos she'd found him staring at her in a way that made her uncomfortably aware of the heaviness of her breasts and the molten heat that pooled between her thighs. That heat was inside her now, flooding through her veins and making each of her nerve endings ultra-sensitive. She was intensely conscious of his hand resting on her bare back. His touch scorched her skin as if he had branded her, and when she stumbled in her high-heeled shoes he increased the pressure of his fingers on her spine and held her so close that she could feel the muscles and sinews of his hard thighs pressed up against hers.

'Sara...look at me.' His voice was low and seductive, scraping across her sensitised nerves. Impossible to resist. She jerked her gaze upwards as if she were a marionette and he had pulled her strings. Her heart lurched as she was trapped by the dark intensity of his eyes. This had been building all week, she realised. Every searing glance they had shared had throbbed with sexual tension that was now threatening to erupt.

His face was so near to hers that she could feel his warm breath graze her lips. She had never been so close to his mouth before and, oh, God, its sensual curve compelled her to lean into him even closer and part her lips, inviting him to cover her mouth with his.

But she must not allow Alekos to kiss her. Certainly not in front of the board members of GE and the senior executives. Her sudden recollection of their situation shattered the spell he had cast on her. It was acceptable for Alekos to dance with his PA, but not to ravish her in public as the sultry gleam in his eyes warned her that he wanted to do.

The band finished playing and Sara took the opportunity to step away from him, murmuring an excuse that she needed to visit the ladies' room. She resisted the urge to glance back at him as she hurried across the dance floor but she felt his dark eyes burning between her shoulder blades, exposed by her backless dress. Luckily, the bathroom was empty and she stood at a basin and held her wrists under the cold tap to try and cool her heated blood. Thank goodness she had stopped him before he had actually kissed her.

The dull ache in the pit of her stomach mocked her for being a liar. She had wanted him to kiss her more than she'd wanted anything in her life. But her common sense reminded her that if he *had*, they would have crossed the line between employer and employee into dangerous territory.

She knew she couldn't put off returning to the party for much longer but she whiled away a few more minutes by checking her phone for messages. Her heart missed a beat when she saw that she had a text from her father.

Five minutes later, Sara stared at her white face in the mirror and willed herself not to cry. Not now, when she must go back and smile and chat to the party guests as her job demanded. She would have to wait until later, when she was alone, before she could allow her tears to fall. She read Lionel's text one more time.

After considerable thought I have decided that it would be unfair to tell Frederick and Charlotte that they have a half-sister at this time. They were very close to their mother and are still mourning her death. The news that many years ago I was unfaithful to my wife will, I fear, be a great shock to my son and daughter. I hope you will understand my decision. It is not my intention to upset you, Sara, but I must protect Freddie and Charlotte and allow them time and privacy to grieve for their mother. Unfortunately, my position as an MP and public figure means that any revelation that I have an illegitimate daughter would attract a great deal of press interest.

In other words, her father had decided that protecting the feelings of the children from his marriage was more important than publicly acknowledging that *she* was his daughter, Sara thought painfully.

Was it because she was as much of a disappointment to her father as she had been to her mother? All her feelings of self-doubt came flooding back. Maybe she wasn't clever enough, or pretty enough, for her famous father.

And maybe, Sara thought grimly, she should have worn the boring black ball gown to the dinner that she'd bought last year specifically to wear to work functions. The dress was a sensible classic style that did not draw attention to her. Instead tonight she'd worn a daring dress that she had secretly hoped would capture Alekos's attention. What had she been hoping for? Did she really want an affair with Alekos when she knew it would mean the end of her job? She'd felt the evidence of his desire for her when he had held her close while they were dancing. But she did not kid herself that his interest in her would last any longer than with his numerous other mistresses.

Alekos wasn't her knight in shining armour. And neither was her father, she acknowledged bleakly. Her mother had taught her that the only person she could rely on was herself. It was a lesson she was determined not to forget.

'Where the hell have you been hiding for the last twenty minutes?' Alekos demanded when Sara joined him at the bar. 'I looked everywhere for you.'

'Why, did you need me for some reason?'

'You should know I need my PA to be on hand at all times,' he growled. While Sara had done her disappearing act from the party he'd been forced to hide behind a pillar to avoid Zelda Pagnotis. Alekos feared no man, but an eighteen-year-old girl who was determined to get her claws into him spelled trouble. Sara sat down on a stool and he wondered if he had imagined that she seemed determined not to make eye contact with him.

'Do you want a drink?' He caught the barman's attention and ordered an orange juice, which he knew was Sara's usual choice of drink.

'Actually, I'd like a whisky and soda, please,' she told the barman. 'Make it a double.'

Alekos gave her a close look and noted her face was pale. Tension emanated from her and he wondered if she was in the grip of the same sexual tension that made his muscles feel tight and his blood thunder through his veins. He had tried to convince himself he'd imagined the chemistry that had simmered between them on the dance floor. But his body clenched as he breathed in her perfume. His reaction to her, the way his manhood jerked to attention beneath his trousers, mocked his assumption that his fascination with her was a temporary aberration.

He frowned when she picked up her glass and threw back her drink in a couple of gulps. 'Is something the matter? You seem on edge.'

'I've got a headache,' she muttered.

'If you didn't before, you soon will have after downing a double whisky,' he said drily.

She slid off the bar stool and picked up her purse. 'Seriously, I...I don't feel well and I need to go home.'

Out of the corner of his eye, Alekos spotted Zelda making her way over to the bar. 'I'll drive you,' he told Sara quickly.

She shook her head. 'I'll call a cab. You don't need to leave the party early on my account.'

'It's fine.' He didn't tell her he was glad of an excuse to leave. 'You are my responsibility and of course I'll take you home if you're not feeling well.'

Alekos had driven himself and Sara to the dinner party in his sports car, and so he hadn't had a drink. As soon as they had escaped the busy roads of central London and reached the motorway he opened up the powerful engine. Twenty minutes later, he turned off into a quiet suburb and drew up outside the nondescript bungalow where she lived.

'Thank you for the lift,' she said when he walked round the car and opened her door.

'No problem.'

On the few previous occasions when he had driven her home, she had asked him in for coffee but he had always declined. Tonight she did not issue an invitation but, perversely, Alekos was curious to see inside

her home, thinking that he might learn more about the
woman who had worked closely with him for two years
but about whom, he realised, he knew very little.

'Goodnight.' Sara turned to walk away from him,
but she caught her heel on an uneven paving slab and
stumbled. *'Ouch.'*

'Are you all right? That's what comes of knocking
back a double whisky when you're not used to drinking spirits,' he told her impatiently.

'I've just twisted my ankle a bit. *Alekos…*' her voice
rose in protest when he scooped her up into his arms
and strode down the garden path to the front door
'…really, it's nothing. I'm fine.'

'Give me your key.'

He heard her mutter something beneath her breath
but she obviously realised it was pointless to argue with
him and dug inside her handbag and gave him a key. He
shifted her in his arms so that he could open the front
door and carried her into the narrow hallway.

'You can put me down now.' She wriggled in an at-
tempt to make him set her on her feet. The friction of
her breasts rubbing against his chest had a predictable
effect on Alekos's body. The hunger he had tried to ignore since he had danced with her at the party ignited
into an inexorable force that burned in his gut.

'You shouldn't walk in high heels if you've sprained
your ankle.'

'I don't suppose it is sprained.' Tension edged into
her voice. 'It was kind of you to bring me home but will
you please go now?'

He ignored her request and continued walking down
the hall, past the sitting room and a small functional
kitchen. Both rooms were painted an insipid beige

which matched the beige carpet. There were two doors on the opposite side of the hall. 'Which is your room?'

'The second door. I can manage now, thanks,' Sara said when he shouldered the door and carried her into her bedroom. She flicked the light switch and Alekos was surprised by the room's décor. The walls were covered with murals of exquisite, brightly coloured flowers and the floral theme extended to the curtains and bedspread. The single bed was piled with stuffed toy bears and a large pink rabbit, which he guessed were relics from her childhood. The room was a vibrant and startling contrast to the otherwise characterless house.

'You obviously like flowers,' he murmured. 'Who painted the murals?'

'I did.'

'Seriously?' He was amazed. 'You're very talented. Did you study art?'

'No,' she said shortly. 'My mother thought I would be wasting my time going to art school. It was her idea that I trained as a secretary because it's a more reliable career.'

Sara wished Alekos would leave. She considered struggling to force him to put her down, but his arms around her were like iron bands and she did not relish an undignified tussle. It was bad enough that he believed she had been affected by alcohol and it was the reason she had tripped and hurt her ankle. He had probably only carried her into the house because he'd felt it was his duty not to leave her sprawled in the gutter. But she did not want him in her bedroom. It was her personal space, and when her mother had been alive it had been the only place where she had been able to indulge the creative side of her nature that she'd recently discovered she had inherited from her father.

Her father who had refused to tell her half-siblings that she was his daughter.

Every word of the text her father had sent her was imprinted on her memory. She told herself it was understandable that Lionel Kingsley cared more about his children from his marriage than for the illegitimate daughter whose existence he had only been aware of for a few months. But it felt like a rejection and it hurt. She had no other family. Her mother had grown up in a children's home, and after Joan had died Sara had felt completely alone until she had met her father.

The tears she'd managed to hold back while she had been at the party filled her eyes and slid down her face. She brushed them away with her hand and swallowed a sob but she felt so empty inside, knowing that she would not now meet her half-brother and half-sister at the weekend. And maybe never, she thought bleakly. Perhaps her father regretted finding out about her.

'Sara, why are you crying? Does your ankle hurt?' Alekos sounded terse. Sara knew he hated displays of emotion as much as she hated displaying her emotions in front of anyone. Even when her mother had died she'd accepted Alekos's rather stilted words of sympathy with quiet dignity and had sensed his relief that she'd kept her emotions out of the office.

But she could not stop crying. Perhaps the whisky she'd drunk at the party had loosened her grip on her self-control. Her father's text had left her utterly bereft and the sense of loneliness that she'd always felt—because she'd never had a strong emotional bond with her mother—now overwhelmed her and she turned her face into Alekos's chest and wept.

Somewhere in her haze of misery she acknowledged that the situation was undoubtedly Alekos's worst nightmare. She remembered an occasion when one of his ex-lovers whom he'd recently dumped had stormed into his office in floods of tears and accused him of breaking her heart. Alekos had literally shuddered in disgust at his ex's undignified behaviour. What must he think of her? Sara wondered. But her tears kept coming. It was as though a dam inside her had burst and allowed her pent-up emotions to escape.

She expected Alekos to stand her on her feet before he beat a hasty retreat from the house. But he didn't. Instead he sat down on the edge of her bed and cradled her in his lap. She was aware of the muscled strength of his arms around her, and the steady beat of his heart that she could hear through his chest was oddly comforting. It was a novelty to feel cared for, even though she knew Alekos's show of tenderness wasn't real. He did not care about her. He'd reminded her when he'd offered to drive her home from the party that she was a member of his staff and therefore his responsibility.

But it was nice to pretend for a few minutes that he actually *meant* the gentle words of comfort he murmured. His voice was softer than she'd ever heard it, and she could almost fool herself that it was the intimate voice of a lover caressing her senses like the brush of velvet against her skin. Gradually her harsh sobs subsided and as she drew a shaky breath she inhaled the spicy musk of Alekos's aftershave mixed with an indefinable male scent that was uniquely him.

In that instant she became conscious of his hard

thighs beneath her bottom and the latent strength of his arms around her. Heat flared inside her and she felt a sensuous heaviness in her breasts and at the molten heart of her femininity.

She could not have said exactly when she sensed a change in him, only that she became aware that his breathing became irregular and his heartbeat beneath her ear quickened and thudded hard and fast. Desire stole through her veins as she lifted her head away from his chest. Her heart lurched when she saw the fierce glitter in his eyes.

'Sara—' His voice throbbed with a raw hunger that made her tremble as she watched him lower his face closer to hers. She stared at his mouth. His sensual, beautiful mouth. So often she had imagined him kissing her with his mouth that promised heaven. 'You're driving me crazy,' he growled before he covered her lips with his and the world went up in flames.

CHAPTER FOUR

HE HAD WANTED to kiss Sara all evening. All week, if he was honest, Alekos admitted to himself, remembering how he had barely been able to keep his hands off her at the office. By the end of each day his gut had felt as if it were tied in a knot, and punishing workouts at the gym after work had failed to relieve his sexual frustration.

There was only one way to assuage the carnal hunger that ignited inside him and made him shake with need. The ache in his groin intensified when Sara parted her lips beneath his and her warm breath filled his mouth. He kissed her the way he'd fantasised about kissing her when he'd first caught sight of her wearing her backless dress. At the party he'd struggled to concentrate on his conversations with the other guests, when all he could think about was running his hands over Sara's naked back. Now he indulged himself and stroked his fingertips up her spine before he clasped her bare shoulders and pulled her even closer to him.

If she had offered the slightest resistance, perhaps he would have come to his senses. But his heart slammed into his ribs when she wound her arms round his neck and threaded her fingers into his hair. Her eager response decimated the last vestiges of his control, and he groaned as he dipped his tongue into her mouth and tasted her. She was nectar, sweet and hot and utterly intoxicating. In the far recesses of his mind Alekos was aware that he should stop this madness. Sara was his secretary, which meant she was off-limits. But it was impossible to associate the beautiful, sensual woman who had driven him to distraction over the past few days with his plain PA who had never warranted a second glance.

She shifted her position on his lap and he groaned again as her bottom ground against his rock-hard erection. He couldn't remember the last time he had felt so turned on. He felt as if he was going to explode and the faint warning voice inside his head was drowned out by the drumbeat of his desire to feel Sara's soft curves beneath him.

He manoeuvred her so that she was lying on the bed and he stretched out on top of her before capturing her mouth once more and kissing her with a deepening hunger that demanded to be appeased. Trailing his lips down her throat, he slid his hand behind her neck into the heavy silk of her hair and discovered that three tiny buttons secured the top of her dress. Three tiny buttons were all that prevented him from pulling the top of her dress down and revealing her ripe breasts that had tantalised him when they had been pressed against his chest. Urgency made his fingers uncooperative. He swore beneath his breath as he struggled to unfasten the buttons and something soft fell across his face.

Lifting his head, Alekos found himself eye to eye with a large pink rabbit. The incongruousness of making love to a woman on a narrow single bed adorned with stuffed animals catapulted him back to reality.

This was not any woman. This was Sara, his efficient, unflappable PA, who apparently had an unexpected liking for cuddly toys. He was only here in her bedroom because she had shockingly burst into tears.

Usually, when faced with a weeping woman, Alekos's instinct was to extricate himself from the situation as quickly possible. But Sara's tears had had an odd effect on him and inexplicably he'd found himself trying to comfort her. He had no idea why she had been crying. But he remembered that in the car when he'd driven her home she had read a text message on her phone and had looked upset.

Memories pushed through the sexual haze that had clouded Alekos's mind. Sara had hurried out of the office at the beginning of the week to meet someone. She had admitted she'd spent her holiday with a male 'friend' at his villa, and she had returned from the French Riviera transformed from a frump into a gorgeous sexpot. At the start of this evening she had seemed happy, but something had happened that had caused her to act out of character and she'd gulped down a double whisky as if it was no stronger than milk.

The most likely explanation Alekos could think of for Sara's distress was that her holiday romance was over. So what the hell was he—*the consolation prize*? He rolled away from her and sat up, assuring himself he was glad he had come to his senses before any harm had been done. Before he'd made the mistake of having sex with her. A kiss was nothing and there was no reason why they couldn't put it behind them and continue with their good working relationship as they had done for the past two years.

He stared at her flushed face and her kiss-stung

mouth that tempted him to forget everything and allow the passion that had sizzled between them moments ago to soar to its natural conclusion. But apart from all the other considerations to them sleeping together—and there were many—Alekos did not relish the idea that Sara wanted someone else and he was second best. *Theos*, he'd spent much of his life feeling second best to his dead brother and believing that, in his father's opinion, he was inferior to Dimitri.

'Alekos.' Sara's soft voice made his gut clench. She sat up and pushed her hair back from her face. She looked as stunned as he felt, and oddly vulnerable. For a moment he had the ridiculous idea that having a man in her bedroom was a new experience for her. 'We...we shouldn't have done that,' she said huskily.

He was well aware of that fact, but he was irritated she had pointed it out. 'It was just a kiss.' He shrugged, as much to emphasise the unimportance of the kiss to himself as well as to her. 'Don't look so stricken, Sara. It won't happen again.' Anger with himself for being so damned weak made him say harshly, 'It wouldn't have happened at all if you hadn't practically begged me to kiss you.'

'I did no such thing.' Fiery colour flared on her cheeks. 'You kissed me. One minute you were comforting me because I was upset, and the next...'

Alekos did not want to think about what had happened next. Remembering how he had explored the moist interior of Sara's mouth with his tongue, and the little moans she had made when he had kissed her, caused his erection to press uncomfortably against the restriction of his trousers.

'Ah, yes, you were upset—' he focused on the first

part of her sentence '—I'm guessing that the reason you were crying was because your holiday lover has dumped you. Your eagerness to kiss me was because you're on the rebound from the guy in France who has rejected you.'

'There was no holiday lover,' she said tightly. 'The "guy in France" was my *father*. I spent my holiday at his villa.' Sara's bottom lip trembled. 'But you're right to think I feel rejected. I'm starting to believe my father regrets that he got in contact with me. Until recently I didn't know about him, or that I have a half-brother and half-sister.' Tears slid down her cheeks. She gave a choked sob and covered her face with her hands, and so did not see Alekos's grim expression.

He had never seen Sara cry until tonight and his abhorrence of emotional displays meant that he really didn't want to stick around. But the fact that she was crying in front of him suggested something serious had happened to upset her. Why, even when she had come to work one Monday morning just before Christmas and told him that her mother had died at the weekend she had kept her emotions in check.

He felt an odd tug in his chest as he watched Sara's body shudder as she tried to regain control of herself. Ignoring a strong temptation to leave her to it, he pulled the dressing table stool next to the bed and sat down on it before he handed her some tissues from the box on the bedside table.

'Thanks,' she said indistinctly. Her tears had washed away most of her make-up, and again Alekos was struck by her air of innocence that he told himself he must have imagined.

'What did you mean when you said you think your

father regrets contacting you? Had there been a rift between the two of you?'

She shook her head. 'It's complicated. I met my father for the first time six weeks ago. When my holiday plans to Spain fell through he invited me to stay at his villa in Antibes. He wasn't there for the whole time, but he came to visit me and we began to get to know each other. I pretended to anyone who asked that I was employed as a housekeeper at the villa because my father was worried about the media.' Her voice broke. 'I'm a scandal from his past, you see, and he doesn't want his other children to find out about me.'

'But why would the media be interested in your father?'

'Because he's famous. I promised I would keep my relationship to him secret until he is ready to publicly acknowledge that I am his illegitimate daughter.'

She was her father's shameful secret, Sara thought miserably. And from the text that Lionel had sent her earlier, it seemed as though she would remain a secret and never meet her half-siblings. She hadn't revealed her father's identity to anyone, not even her closest friend, Ruth, who she had known since they were at primary school. But the truth about her father that at first had been such a wonderful surprise had become a burden she longed to share with someone.

She blinked away yet more tears. Her head ached from crying and she wished she could rest it on the pillows. But if she did that, Alekos might think she was inviting him to lie on the bed with her and kiss her again. She darted a glance at him and heat ran through her veins as she remembered the weight of him pressing her into the mattress and the feel of his muscular thighs as he'd ground his hips against her pelvis.

Of course she hadn't 'practically begged him to kiss her', as he'd accused her, she assured herself. But she hadn't stopped him. She bit her lip. Alekos had been the one to draw back, and if he hadn't... The tugging sensation in the pit of her stomach became a sharp pull of need as her imagination ran riot and she pictured them both naked, their limbs entwined and his body joined with hers.

She flushed as her eyes crashed into his glittering dark gaze and she realised that he was aware she had been staring at him.

'Why did you only meet your father for the first time recently?'

'He wasn't part of my life when I was growing up.' She shrugged to show him it didn't hurt, even though it did. 'My mother was employed as my father's secretary when they had an affair. He was married with a family, but he decided that he wanted to try and save his marriage and ended his relationship with Mum. She moved away without telling him that she was pregnant. She refused to talk about him and I have no idea why, in the last week of her life, she wrote to him and told him about me.'

She sighed. 'My father found out about me six months ago, but his wife was ill and he waited until after she had died before he phoned and asked if we could meet. He said he was glad he had found me. He'd assumed that my mother had told me his identity. Now I'm wondering if his reason for finding me was because he feared I might sell the story about my famous father to the newspapers. If the press got hold of the story it could damage his relationship with his children from his marriage. And I imagine the scandal that he'd had an affair, even though it was years ago, might harm his political career.'

Alekos's brows rose. 'Your father is a politician?'

Sara felt torn between her promise to protect her father's identity and what she told herself was a selfish need to unburden her secret to *someone*. But to Alekos? Strangely, he was the one person she trusted above all others. The tabloids made much of his playboy reputation, but she knew another side to him. He was dedicated to GE and worked hard to make it a globally successful business. He was a tough but fair employer and he was intensely protective of his mother and sisters. He guarded his own privacy fiercely, but could she trust that he would guard hers?

'It's vital that the story isn't leaked to the media,' she cautioned.

'You know my feelings about the scum who are fondly known as the paparazzi,' he said sardonically. 'I'm not likely to divulge anything you tell me in confidence to the press.'

She snatched a breath. 'My father is Lionel Kingsley.' It was the first time she had ever said the words aloud and it felt strange. Alekos looked shocked and she wondered if she had been naïve to confide in him. Now he knew something about her that no one else knew, and for some reason that made her feel vulnerable.

He gave a low whistle. 'Do you mean the Right Honourable Lionel Kingsley, MP—the Minister for Culture and the Arts? I've met him on a few occasions, both socially and also in his capacity as Culture Secretary, when I sponsored an exhibition of Greek art at the British Museum. As a matter of fact he was a guest at a party I went to earlier this week.'

'It sounds as though you have a lot more in common with my father than I do,' Sara muttered. She didn't move in the exalted social circles that Alekos and Lionel did, and she would definitely never have the opportunity to meet her father or her half-siblings socially. She tried to focus on what Alekos was saying.

'What has happened to make you think your father regrets finding you?'

'I was supposed to go and stay at his home at the weekend so that I could meet my half-siblings. But Lionel has decided against telling Freddie and Charlotte about me. It's only two months since their mother died. They were very close to her, and he's worried about how they will react to the news that he had been unfaithful to his wife.'

She pressed her hand to her temple, which had started to throb. 'I get the impression that I'm a complication and Lionel wishes he hadn't told me he is my father. His name isn't on my birth certificate and there's no possibility I could have found out I'm his daughter.'

She swung her legs off the bed and stood up. Alekos also got to his feet and her small bedroom seemed to be dominated by his six-feet-plus of raw masculinity.

'You should go,' she said abruptly, feeling too strung out to play the role of polite hostess. 'What happened just now…when we kissed…' her face flamed when he said nothing but looked amused, damn him '…obviously it can never happen again. I mean, you have a strict rule about not sleeping with your staff. Not that I'm suggesting you want to sleep with me,' she added quickly, in case he thought she was hinting that she hoped he wanted to have an affair with her.

Hot with embarrassment, she ploughed on, 'It was an unfortunate episode and I blame my behaviour on the whisky I drank earlier.'

'Rubbish.' Alekos laughed softly. 'You're not drunk. And I haven't had a drink all night. Alcohol had nothing to do with why we kissed. It was chemistry that ignited between us and made us both act out of character.'

'Exactly.' Sara seized on his words. 'It was a mistake, and the best thing we can do is to forget it happened.'

He deliberately lowered his eyes to her breasts, and she fought the temptation to cross her arms over her chest and hide her nipples that she was aware had hardened and must be visible jutting beneath the silky material of her dress. Somehow she made herself look at him calmly.

'Do you think it will be possible to forget the passion that exploded between us?' he murmured.

'It has to be, if I am going to continue as your PA.' She sounded fiercer than she had intended as she fought a rising sense of panic that the memory of Alekos kissing her would stay in her mind for a very long time. 'And now I really would like you to leave. It's late, and I'm tired.'

He checked his watch and said in an amused voice, 'It's a quarter to ten, which is hardly late. We left the dinner early because you said you were feeling unwell.'

To her relief he said no more and walked over to the door. 'I'll see myself out. And Sara—' his gaze held hers and his tone was suddenly serious '—your secret is safe with me. For what it's worth, I think your father should feel very proud to have you as his daughter.'

Alekos's unexpected compliment was the last straw for Sara's battered emotions. She held on until she heard the front door bang as he closed it behind him before she gave in to the tears that had threatened her composure since he had *stopped* kissing her.

Yes, she was upset about her father, but she was horrified to admit that she was more hurt by Alekos's rejection. She couldn't forget that he had been the one who had come to his senses. But what did her tears say about her? Why was she crying over a man who hadn't paid her any attention for two years? He had only noticed her recently because she'd revamped her appearance.

Alekos's interest in her was a passing fancy, but he could very easily break her heart if she allowed him to. She wished she *had* been drunk tonight, she brooded. At least then she could forgive herself for responding to him the way she had. Instead she only had her foolish heart to blame.

It took all of Sara's willpower to make herself stroll into Alekos's office the next morning and give him a cheerful smile before she turned her attention to the espresso machine.

His eyes narrowed when she walked over to his desk and placed a cup of coffee in front of him. She had resisted the urge to wear the beige dress that still lurked in the back of her wardrobe—a remnant of her previous dreary style. Out of sheer bravado she had chosen a bright red skirt and a red-and-white polka-dot blouse. Red stilettos and a slick of scarlet lip gloss completed her outfit. Her layered hairstyle flicked the tops of her shoulders as she sat down composedly and waited for him to give her instructions for the day.

'You're looking very perky. I trust you are feeling better?'

The gleam in his dark eyes was almost her undoing, but she had promised herself that she wouldn't let him rattle her and so she smiled and said coolly, 'Much better, thank you. I'm just sorry that you had to leave the dinner early last night because of me.'

'I'm not,' he murmured. The gleam turned to something darker and hotter as he skimmed his gaze down from her pink cheeks to her dotty blouse, and Sara was sure he was remembering the passion that had exploded between them in her bedroom.

She was conscious of the pulse at the base of her throat beating erratically and said hurriedly, 'Shall we get on? I thought you wanted to go through the final details for the Monaco Yacht Show.'

Alekos's sardonic smile told her he had seen through her distraction ploy, but to her relief he opened the folder in front of him. 'As you know, GE is one of the top exhibitors at the show, and we will be using the company's show yacht to give tours and demonstrations to potential clients interested in buying a superyacht. I've heard from the captain of *Artemis* that she has docked in Monaco and the crew are preparing her for the show. You and I will fly out to meet the rest of the sales team, and we will stay on board the yacht.'

For the rest of the morning, work was the only topic of conversation and if Sara tried hard she could almost pretend that the events of the previous night hadn't happened. It helped if she didn't look directly at Alekos but on the occasions when she did make eye contact with him the glittering heat in his gaze caused her stomach to dip. Alekos had called it *chemistry*, and its tangible presence every time she stepped into his office simmered between them and filled the room with a prickling tension that seemed to drain the air from Sara's lungs.

She was relieved when he left for a lunch appointment and told her he did not expect to be back until later in the afternoon. But, perversely, once he had gone she missed him and couldn't settle down to her work because she kept picturing his ruggedly handsome face and reliving the feel of his lips on hers. It was just a kiss, she reminded herself. But deep down she knew that something fundamental had changed between her and Alekos. She had hidden her feelings for him for two years, but it was so much harder to hide her desire for him when he looked at her with a hungry gleam in his eyes that made her ache with longing.

He returned just before five o'clock and seemed surprised to find her still at her desk. 'I thought you wanted to leave early tonight.'

'I'm not going to visit my father at his home in Berkshire now, so I thought I might as well catch up on some filing,' she said in a carefully controlled voice. She was embarrassed that she had cried in front of Alekos last night and was determined to hide her devastation over her father's change of heart about introducing her to her half-siblings.

His speculative look gave her the unsettling notion that he could read her thoughts. 'I've been thinking about your situation and I have an idea of how to help. Come into my office. I'm sure you would rather not discuss a personal matter where anyone walking past could overhear us.'

Sara didn't want to have a personal discussion with him anywhere, but he held open his office door and she could not think of an excuse to refuse. Besides, she was intrigued that he had actually thought about her. 'What idea?' she said as soon as he had shut the door.

He walked around his desk and waited until she was seated opposite him before he replied. 'On Sunday evening I have been invited to the launch of a new art gallery in Soho.'

'I'm up to speed with your diary, Alekos.' She hid her disappointment that he had brought her in to discuss his busy social schedule. But why would he be interested in her problems?

He ignored her interruption. 'The gallery's owner, Jemima Wilding, represents several well-established artists, but she also wants to support new talent and the gallery's launch will include paintings by an up-and-coming artist, Freddie Kingsley.'

Sara's heart gave an odd thump. 'I didn't know that my half-brother was an artist.'

'I believe Freddie and Charlotte both studied art at Chelsea College of Art. Charlotte is establishing herself as a fashion designer. She will be at the gallery launch on Sunday to support her brother, along with Lionel Kingsley.'

'Why are you telling me this?' She could not keep the bitterness from her voice. Alekos was emphasising what she already knew—that she did not belong in the rarefied world that her father and half-siblings, and Alekos himself, occupied.

'Because my idea is that you could accompany me to

the gallery launch to meet your half-siblings. I realise you won't be able to say that you are related to them, but you might have a chance to talk to your father in private during the evening and persuade him to reveal your true identity.'

Her heart gave another lurch as she tried to imagine meeting Freddie and Charlotte. Would they notice the physical similarities she shared with them? Probably not, she reassured herself. They were unaware that they had an illegitimate half-sister. Alekos was offering her what might be her only opportunity to meet her blood relations. Common sense doused her excitement. 'It would look strange if you took your PA to a private engagement.'

'Possibly, but you wouldn't be there as my PA. You would accompany me as my date. My mistress,' he explained when she stared at him uncomprehendingly.

For a third time Sara's heart jolted against her ribs. 'We agreed to forget about the kiss we shared last night.' She flushed, hating how she sounded breathless when she had intended her voice to be cool and crisp.

His eyes gleamed like hot coals for a second before the fire in those dark depths was replaced by a faintly cynical expression that Sara was more used to seeing. 'I don't remember agreeing to forget about it,' he drawled. 'But I'm suggesting that we *pretend* to be in a relationship. If people believe you are my girlfriend it will seem perfectly reasonable for you to be with me.'

'I can see a flaw in your plan.' Several flaws, as it happened, but she focused on the main one. 'You have made it clear that you would never become personally involved with any member of your staff. If we are seen together in public it's likely that the board members of

GE will believe we are having an affair. They disapprove of your playboy reputation and might even decide to take a vote of no confidence against you.'

'That won't happen. As you said yourself, the board members approve of you. They think you are a good, stabilising influence on me,' he said drily.

Sara remembered the many glamorous blondes Alekos had dated in the past. 'I'm not sure your friends would be convinced that you and I are in a relationship,' she said doubtfully.

'They'd have been convinced if they had seen us together last night.' His wicked grin made her blush. 'The plan will work because of the sexual chemistry between us. There's no point in denying it.' He did not give her a chance to speak. 'It is an inconvenient attraction that we might as well use to our advantage.'

So she was an inconvenience! It was hardly a flattering description. 'Why are you willing to help me meet my half-siblings? You've never taken an interest in my personal life before.'

He shrugged. 'You're right to guess I am not being entirely altruistic. Zelda Pagnotis will also be at the gallery launch. She is a friend of Jemima Wilding's daughter, Leah. You saw how Zelda followed me around at the board members' dinner, how she changed the name cards around so that she was seated next to me.' Frustration clipped his voice. 'Her crush on me is becoming a problem, but if she believes that you are my girlfriend it might persuade her to move her attention onto another guy.'

'Are you saying you need me to protect you from Zelda?'

'Orestis thinks I want to corrupt his granddaughter,'

Alekos growled. 'Of course nothing could be further from the truth, but I guarantee Orestis won't disapprove of you being my mistress. He's more likely to be relieved.'

'But why don't you flaunt a genuine mistress in front of Zelda? There must be dozens of women who would jump at the chance to go on a date with you.'

'I don't happen to have a girlfriend at the moment. If I invite one of my exes to the gallery launch there's a risk they will read too much into it and believe I want to get back with them.'

'What it is to be Mr Popular,' Sara murmured wryly. Alekos's arrogance was infuriating, but he had a point. In the two years that she had been his PA she'd realised that women threw themselves at him without any encouragement from him.

He hadn't needed to encourage her to kiss him last night. She flushed as she remembered how eagerly she had responded to him. But he had called a halt to their passion even though he must have sensed that she wanted him to make love to her. Now he was asking her to pretend to be in love with him, and she was afraid she would be too convincing.

'What do you think of my idea, Sara? It seems to me that it will be an ideal solution for both of us.'

She looked into his dark eyes and her heart gave a familiar swoop. 'I need time to think about it.'

He frowned. 'How much time? I'll need to let Jemima know that I am bringing a guest.'

Sara refused to let him browbeat her into making a decision. Although she longed to meet her half-siblings she was worried about how her father might react to seeing her at a social event. 'Phone me in the morning and I'll give you my answer,' she said calmly. She stood up and walked over to the door, but then hesitated and turned to look at him.

'Thank you for offering to help me meet my half-siblings. I appreciate it.'

Alekos waited until Sara had closed the door behind her before he strode over to the drinks cabinet and poured himself a double measure of malt Scotch. Her smile had hit him like a punch in his gut. He'd always known he was a bastard, and Sara had confirmed it when she'd said that she appreciated his help.

He raked his hair off his brow. Sara had no idea that her revelation about her father's identity was a very useful piece of knowledge that he intended to use to his advantage. His keenness to attend the gallery launch had nothing to do with an interest in art and everything to do with business. Alekos knew that the Texan oil billionaire Warren McCuskey was on the guest list. He also knew that McCuskey and Lionel Kingsley were close friends.

The story went that many years ago both men had been amateur sailors competing in a transatlantic yacht race, but the American had nearly lost his life when his boat had capsized. Lionel Kingsley had been leading the race but had sacrificed his chance of winning when he'd gone to McCuskey's assistance. Three decades later, Warren McCuskey had become one of the richest men in the US and the person who had the most influence over him was his good friend, English politician Lionel Kingsley—who, astonishingly, happened to be Sara's father.

Alekos was aware that networking was a crucial part

of business, and the best deals were forged at social events where the champagne flowed freely. He'd heard that McCuskey was considering splashing out some of his huge fortune on a superyacht. At the party on Sunday evening, Sara would want to spend time with her father, and it would be an ideal opportunity for him to ingratiate himself with the Texan billionaire.

He took a swig of his Scotch and ignored the twinge of his conscience as he thought of Sara and how he planned to use a fake affair with her for his own purpose. All was fair in love and business, he thought sardonically. Not that he knew anything about love. GE was his top priority and he had a responsibility, a *duty*, to ensure that the company was as successful as it would undoubtedly have been under Dimitri's leadership. He secretly suspected that his brother had thrown his life away because of a woman. But Alekos would never allow any woman close to his heart and certainly not to influence his business strategy.

CHAPTER FIVE

THE LIMOUSINE CAME to a halt beside the kerb and Alekos prepared to step out of the car, when Sara's voice stopped him.

'I don't think I can go through with it.' Her voice shook. 'You didn't say the press would be here.'

He glanced out of the window at the group of journalists and cameramen gathered on the pavement outside the Wilding Gallery. 'There was bound to be some media interest. Jemima Wilding is well-known in the art world and naturally she wants exposure for her new gallery. I suspect she leaked the names on the guest list to the paparazzi,' he said drily.

The chauffeur opened the door but Sara did not move. 'Doesn't it bother you that photos of us arriving together might be published in the newspapers and give the impression that we are…a couple?'

'But that's the point.' Alekos stifled his impatience, realising he needed to reassure her. When he'd phoned Sara on Saturday morning, she had said she would pretend to be his mistress and accompany him to the gallery launch. Now she seemed to be having second thoughts. 'You want to meet your half-siblings, don't you?' he reminded her of the reason she had agreed to his plan.

'Of course I do. But I'm worried my father will be angry when he sees me. He might think I came here tonight to put pressure on him to tell Charlotte and Freddie about me.'

'Then we will have to put on a convincing act that you are my girlfriend and you are at the party with me.'

'I suppose so.' She still sounded unsure. Alekos watched her sink her teeth into her soft lower lip and was tempted to soothe the maligned flesh with his tongue. But such an action, although undoubtedly enjoyable, would be wasted here in the car where they couldn't be seen.

Glancing out of the window again, he noticed a young woman, wearing a skirt so short it was not much more than a belt, standing in the glass-fronted lobby of the gallery. He gritted his teeth. Zelda Pagnotis was an irritating thorn in his side, but unless he took drastic action to end her crush on him the teenager could become a more serious problem and cause a further rift between him and her grandfather.

'Thank you, Mike,' Alekos said to the chauffeur as he climbed out of the car and held out his hand to Sara. After a few seconds' hesitation she put her fingers in his and stepped onto the pavement. She stiffened when he slid his arm around her waist and escorted her over to the entrance of the art gallery. As Alekos had predicted, the paparazzi took pictures of him and Sara, and she pressed closer to him and put her head down as the flashbulbs went off around them when they walked into the building.

A doorman stepped forwards to take her coat. It had been raining earlier when the car had collected her from her house and Alekos hadn't seen what she was wearing beneath her raincoat until now.

Theos! He tore his eyes from her and glanced around him, thinking he had spoken out loud. But no one was looking at him. He returned his gaze to her and stared. 'Your dress...'

'Is it all right?' Her tongue darted out to moisten her lips. The gesture betrayed her nervousness and sent a shaft of white-hot desire through Alekos. 'Is my dress suitable?' she said in an undertone. 'Why are you staring at me?'

'It's more than suitable. You look incredible.' He ran his eyes over her bare shoulders, revealed by her emerald silk strapless dress, down to the rounded curves of her breasts that made him think of ripe peaches, firm and delicately flushed, tempting him to taste them. Lowering his gaze still further, he noted how the design of the dress drew attention to her slim waist before the skirt flared over her hips and fell to just above her knees.

Forcing his eyes back up her body, he noted how her layered hair swirled around her shoulders when she turned her head, and the hot ache in his groin intensified when he imagined her silky hair brushing across his naked chest as he lifted her on top of him and guided her down onto his hard shaft.

'Theos.' This time he spoke aloud in a rough voice as he curved his hand behind her neck and drew her towards him. He saw her eyes widen until they were huge green pools that pulled him in.

'Alekos,' she whispered warningly, as if to remind him that they were not alone in the lobby. But she didn't pull away as he lowered his face towards hers.

'Sara,' he mocked softly. And then he covered her mouth with his and kissed her, long and slow, and then deep and hard when she parted her lips and kissed him back with a sweet intensity that made his gut twist and made him want to sweep her up in his arms and carry her off to somewhere where they could be alone.

The low murmur of voices pushed into his consciousness and he reluctantly lifted his head and snatched oxygen into his lungs. Sara looked as stunned as he felt, but he had no intention of admitting that what had just happened was a first for him. He had *never* kissed a woman in public before. As he stepped away from her he caught sight of Zelda Pagnotis hurrying out of the lobby wearing a sulky expression on her face.

'First objective of the evening completed,' he told Sara smoothly, keen to hide the effect she had on him. 'Zelda can't doubt that we are having an affair. I've just spotted Lionel Kingsley and his son and daughter. Are you ready to meet your half-siblings?'

Sara could feel her heart hammering beneath her ribs as she walked with Alekos into the main gallery. She was excited that in a few moments she would meet her half-brother and half-sister for the first time, but she was still reeling from the sizzling kiss she had shared with Alekos.

While she'd been in his arms she had forgotten where they were, or why he had brought her to the art gallery. But when he had lifted his mouth from hers, she'd seen Zelda Pagnotis walk past them and realised that Alekos had deliberately kissed her in view of the teenager. *First objective completed.* She recalled his words ruefully. What an idiot she was to have believed that he'd kissed her because he desired her.

She looked ahead to the group of people Alekos was heading towards and her heart beat harder when she saw her father. Lionel was frowning as he watched her approach and her hesitant smile faltered. *She shouldn't have come*. The last thing she wanted to do was alienate her father. Her steps slowed and she felt a strong urge to run out of the gallery, but Alekos slipped his arm around her waist and propelled her forwards.

A tall woman with purple hair detached from the group and greeted them. 'Alekos, darling, I'm so glad you were able to come this evening. That was quite an entrance you made,' she said in an amused voice that made Sara blush. 'You must be Sara. I'm Jemima Wilding. I'm so pleased to meet you. Alekos, I think you and Lionel Kingsley have met before.'

'We have indeed.' Lionel shook Alekos's hand. 'Your financial support of the Greek art exhibition last year was much appreciated. But actually we met very recently at a party earlier this week.' He glanced at Alekos's hand resting on Sara's waist. 'You were unaccompanied on that occasion.'

'Yes, unfortunately Sara had another commitment,' Alekos said smoothly. He tightened his arm around Sara's waist as if he guessed that her heart was fluttering like a trapped bird in her chest. 'This is Sara Lovejoy.'

To Sara, the silence seemed to last for ever and stretched her nerves to the snapping point. But in reality Lionel Kingsley hesitated infinitesimally before he shook her hand. 'I am delighted to meet you... Miss Lovejoy.'

'Sara,' she said thickly. Her throat felt constricted and she smiled gratefully at Alekos when he handed her a flute of champagne from a passing waiter.

Lionel introduced the other people in the group, starting with a stockily built man with a rubicund face. 'This is my good friend Warren McCuskey, who flew to London from Texas especially so that he could attend the gallery launch and support my son Freddie's first exhibition.'

Sara greeted Warren with a polite smile, but her heart was thumping as Freddie Kingsley stretched his hand towards her. She prayed no one would notice her hand was trembling as she held it out to him.

Her half-brother smiled. 'Pleased to meet you, Sara.'

'I...' Emotion clogged her throat as Freddie closed his fingers around hers. His handshake was firm and his skin felt warm beneath her fingertips. Her secret drummed in her brain. Freddie was unaware that the blood running through his veins was partly the same as her blood. She swallowed and tried to speak but the lump in her throat prevented her.

Alekos moved imperceptibly closer, as if he understood that her emotions were balanced on a knife-edge. There was something comforting about his big-framed, solid presence at her side and, to her relief, she could suddenly breathe again.

'It's lovely to meet you,' she told Freddie softly. Her half-brother was taller than she had imagined, his brown hair curled over his collar and his smile was wide and welcoming. She looked into his green eyes and recognised herself.

He gave her a puzzled look. 'Have we met before? Your face seems familiar.'

'No, we've never met.' Sara was conscious of her father standing a few feet away and wondered if she was the only person in the group who could sense Lionel's tension.

Freddie shrugged. 'You definitely remind me of someone but I can't think who. Are you interested in art, Sara?'

'Very. I'd love to see your work.'

She followed Freddie over to where six of his paintings were displayed against a white wall. Even to her untrained eye she could tell that he was a gifted artist. His use of intense colour and light made his landscapes bold and exciting.

'My brother is very talented, isn't he?'

Sara turned her head towards the voice and discovered her half-sister standing next to her.

'I'm Charlotte Kingsley, by the way. I really like your dress.' Charlotte grinned and murmured, 'I really like your gorgeous boyfriend too. And he seems very keen on you. Even when he is talking to other people he can't keep his eyes off you. Have the two of you been together long?'

'Um...not that long.' Sara experienced the same difficulty speaking that had happened when she'd met Freddie. She felt an instant connection with Charlotte which made her think that maybe they could become friends. But perhaps her half-siblings would hate her if they learned that she was the result of Lionel Kingsley's affair with her mother.

She chatted for a few minutes and then slipped away to a quiet corner of the gallery, needing to be alone with her churning emotions. It was obvious that Charlotte and Freddie were deeply fond of each other. Sara felt a pang of envy as she watched them laughing together. Her childhood had been lonely because her mother hadn't encouraged her to invite school friends home. She had longed for a brother or sister to be a companion, unaware that growing up in Berkshire had been her half-sister, who was a year older than her, and her half-brother, three years her senior.

Tears gathered in her eyes and she quickly blinked them away when Lionel walked over to join her. She glanced around the gallery, searching for Alekos. Her instinctive need for his protection was a danger that she would have to deal with later. She saw him chatting with the Texan, Warren McCuskey, and her heart gave a silly skip as she realised that Alekos must have purposely given her and her father a few minutes of privacy.

'Sara, it's good to see you.' Lionel's smile allayed her concern that he was annoyed she had come to the party. 'I had no idea you were dating Alekos Gionakis. I thought you worked for him?'

'I'm his PA, but recently we…we've become close.' She felt her face grow warm. Lying did not come naturally to her. But she had to admit that Alekos's idea for her to pretend to be his girlfriend had allowed her to meet her half-siblings, and maybe she had a chance of persuading her father to reveal her identity to Freddie and Charlotte.

'Gionakis is an interesting man. He is knowledgeable of the arts but I've heard that he's a ruthless businessman.' Lionel lowered his voice so that he couldn't be overheard by anyone else. 'Sara, if Joan had told me she was pregnant I would have offered her financial support while you were a child. I regret that you did not grow up in a family.'

'I have a half-brother and half-sister who are my family, and I would love to get to know Charlotte and Freddie if only you would tell them I am your daughter,' Sara replied in a fierce whisper.

Her father looked uncomfortable. 'I will tell them when the time is right. Maybe if they got to know you first it would help when I break the news that I once cheated on their mother.' He looked round and saw Alekos approaching. 'Does Gionakis know of our relationship?'

Sara hesitated. 'Yes. But I know Alekos won't say a word to anyone,' she said hurriedly when Lionel frowned.

'You must love him to trust him so much.'

Love Alekos! Sara found she could not refute her father's comment. Her heart gave a familiar lurch as she watched Alekos walk towards her. He looked outrageously sexy, wearing a casual but impeccably tailored light grey suit and a black shirt, unbuttoned at the neck. His thick hair was ruffled as if he'd raked it off his brow several times during the evening, and the dark stubble shading his jaw added to his dangerous magnetism.

Of course she was in love with him; she finally admitted what she had tried to deny to herself for two years. She loved Alekos, but he'd told her he did not believe in love. Just because you loved someone didn't mean you could make them love you back. Her mother had discovered the truth of that when she had fallen in love with Lionel Kingsley.

'I told you my plan would work.' Alekos knew he sounded smug but he didn't care. He'd had a couple of drinks at the gallery launch and, although he was certainly not drunk, he felt relaxed and pleased with how the evening had gone. He leaned his head against the plush leather back seat of the limousine as they sped towards north London. His thoughts were on Warren McCuskey. The Texan billionaire was definitely interested in buying a superyacht and Alekos had used all his persuasive powers to convince him to commission a yacht from GE. He was confident he was close to finalising a deal with McCuskey. He could taste success, smell it.

He could also smell Sara's perfume. The blend of citrusy bergamot and sensual white musk, that had tantalised him every day at the office, filled the dark car and his senses. Suddenly he didn't feel relaxed any more. He felt wired up inside, the way Sara always made him feel lately. He was conscious of the hard thud of his heart and the even harder ache of his arousal that jerked to attention and pushed against the zip of his trousers.

'I don't think Zelda will continue to be a problem now that she believes you are my mistress,' he drawled, more to remind himself of the reason why he had spent most of the evening with his arm around Sara's waist. She'd fitted against his side as if she belonged there. He frowned as he remembered how, every time he'd leaned towards her, he'd inhaled a vanilla scent in her hair that he guessed was the shampoo she used.

'Good. That's one problem solved at least.' She sounded distracted.

Alekos glanced at her sitting beside him. She had put her coat on before they'd left the gallery, but it was undone and he could see the smooth upper slopes of her breasts above the top of her dress. 'Is there another problem?' he said abruptly.

'There might be.' She flicked her head round to look at him and her hair brushed against his shoulder, leaving a trail of vanilla scent. 'Alekos, we need to talk.'

Talking to Sara was not uppermost in his mind. But if he told her of his erotic thoughts about her she would probably slap his face. The car pulled up outside her house. 'Invite me in for coffee and you can tell me what's troubling you.'

'All right,' she said after a moment's hesitation. 'But I only have instant coffee. Will that do?'

As Alekos followed her into the house he regretted his suggestion. He detested the insipid brown liquid that the English insisted on calling coffee. But, more pertinently, he couldn't understand why he had suggested to Sara that she could confide in him what he assumed was a problem with her private life. He was about to tell her not to worry about the coffee but she showed him into the sitting room, saying, 'I'll go and put the kettle on.'

It was difficult to imagine a room more characterless than the one he was standing in. The neutral décor was joyless, as if whoever had chosen the beige furnishings had found no pleasure in life. It was a strangely oppressive room and Alekos retreated and walked down the bungalow's narrow hallway to the kitchen.

Sara had taken off her coat and she looked like a gaudy butterfly in her bright dress against the backdrop of sterile worktops and cupboards. She had also slipped off her shoes and he was struck by how petite she was without her high heels. The sight of her bare feet with her toenails varnished a flirty shade of pink had an odd effect on him and he felt his gut twist with desire. He searched for something to say while he struggled to control his rampant libido.

'How come your bedroom is so colourful, while the rest of the house is...' he swapped the word *drab* for '...plain?'

'My mother didn't like bright colours. Now Mum has gone I've decided to sell the house. The estate agent advised me not to redecorate because buyers prefer a blank canvas.' She placed a mug on the counter in front of him. 'I made your coffee extra strong so it should taste like freshly ground coffee.'

Alekos thought it was highly unlikely. But remembering Sara's brightly coloured bedroom brought back memories of his previous visit to her home when he had kissed her and passion had ignited between them. There was barely enough space for the two of them in the tiny kitchen but he didn't want to suggest they move into the sitting room, which was as welcoming as a morgue. He sipped his coffee and managed not to grimace. 'What did you want to talk about?'

'Lionel thinks it would be a good idea if I could mix with Charlotte and Freddie socially so they can get to know me before he tells them I am their half-sister. He intends to use his association with you—namely your support of art projects—to invite us both to his villa in Antibes, where he's planning to celebrate his birthday.' Sara tugged on her bottom lip with her small white teeth, sending Alekos quietly to distraction as he imagined covering her lush mouth with his.

'Go on,' he muttered.

'I couldn't tell my father that I had pretended to be your girlfriend tonight so I could meet my half-siblings. Lionel believes we are genuinely in a relationship and we would have to continue the pretence if you accept his invitation.'

'Who else has your father invited to his villa?'

'Charlotte and Freddie and my father's close friend Warren McCuskey. By the way, thanks for chatting to Warren at the gallery while I spoke to my father privately.'

'You're welcome.' Alekos ignored the irritating voice of his conscience, which reminded him he was an unprincipled bastard. It was a fact of life that you couldn't head a multimillion-pound business and have principles. He'd seized his chance to grab McCuskey's undivided attention while Sara was talking to Lionel. 'When is your father's birthday?'

'Next weekend. I'd mentioned that we will be in Monaco for the yacht show and he said that Antibes is only about an hour's drive away. But I did warn him that we will be busy with the show and might not have time to visit him.'

'Our schedule for the three days of the show is hectic. But how about if I arranged a birthday lunch for your father and his guests aboard *Artemis* for next Sunday? That way we can catch up on paperwork in the morning, and you'll be able to spend time with Lionel and your brother and sister in the afternoon.' It would also be an ideal opportunity to give Warren McCuskey a demonstration of GE's flagship superyacht, but Alekos kept that to himself.

'Would you really be prepared to do that on my behalf?' Her smile stole his breath and he shrugged off the niggling voice of his conscience. Sara caught her lower lip between her teeth again. 'But will you mind having to keep up the pretence that I am your girlfriend?'

Alekos dropped his gaze from her mouth to the delectable creamy curves of her breasts cupped in her silk dress, and he was surprised that the thud of his heart wasn't audible. 'I think I can put up with pretending that we are lovers,' he drawled.

He smiled when he heard her breath rush from her lungs as he wrapped his arm around her waist and drew her towards him so that she was pressed against his chest, against his heat and the hardness of his arousal that ached. *Theos,* he had never ached so badly for a woman before.

'Alekos,' she whispered. Her green eyes were very dark and he saw her uncertainty reflected in their depths as he lowered his head. 'What are you doing?'

'Rehearsing for when we meet your father,' he growled before he slanted his mouth over hers and kissed her like he'd wanted to do, like he'd been burning up to do since he had kissed her in the lobby of the art gallery. The difference was that that had been for Zelda Pagnotis's sake, or so Alekos had assured himself. But this time it was lust, pure and simple, that made him cup Sara's jaw in his palm and angle her head so that he could plunder her lips and slide his tongue into her mouth to taste her sweetness.

Without her high-heeled shoes she was much smaller than him and Alekos lifted her up and sat her on the kitchen worktop, nudging her thighs apart so that he could stand between them. The fact that she let him gave him the licence he needed to capture her mouth and kiss her again, hard this time, demanding her response as the fire inside him burned out of control.

Her shoulders were silky smooth beneath his hands. He traced his fingers along the delicate line of her collarbone before moving lower to explore the upper slopes of her breasts. Touching wasn't enough. He had to see her, had to cradle those firm mounds in his hands. With his lips still clinging to hers, he reached behind her and unzipped her dress. The green silk bodice slipped down and he helped it on its way, tugging the material until her breasts popped free. His breath hissed between his teeth as he feasted his eyes on her bare breasts, so pale against his tanned fingers, and at their centre her nipples, tight and dusky pink, just waiting for his tongue to caress them.

With a low growl Alekos lowered his mouth to her breast and drew wet circles around the areola before he closed his lips on her nipple and sucked. The soft cry she gave turned him on even more and he slid his arms around her back and encouraged her to arch her body and offer her breasts to his mouth. Every flick of his tongue across her nipple sent a shudder of response through her and when he transferred his attention to her other breast and sucked the tender peak she made a keening noise and dug her fingers into his hair as if to hold him to his task of pleasuring her.

He was so hard it hurt. His erection strained beneath his trousers as he shifted even closer to her, forcing her to spread her legs wider so that her dress rode up her thighs and he pressed his hardness against the panel of her knickers. Knowing that a fragile strip of lace was all that hid her feminine core from him shattered the last of his restraint and he groaned and cupped her face in his hands.

'Let's go to bed, Sara *mou*. This kitchen is not big enough for me to make love to you comfortably.' He doubted that her single bed would offer much more in the way of comfort and remembering her collection of child's soft toys strewn on her bed was a little off-putting. But the only other room was that soulless sitting room and he quickly dismissed the idea of having sex with her there.

He eased back from her and looked down at her naked breasts with their reddened, swollen nipples. 'Come with me,' he said urgently. If he did not have her soon he would explode.

Bed! Sara stiffened as Alekos's thick voice broke through the haze of sexual excitement he had created with his mouth and his wicked tongue. When he had sucked her nipples she'd felt an electrical current arc from her breasts down to the molten core of her femininity. She'd been spellbound by his magic, enthralled by the myriad new sensations induced by his increasingly bold caresses. But his words brought her back to reality with a thud.

On the opposite wall of the kitchen she could see her reflection in the stainless steel cooker splashback that her mother had religiously polished until it gleamed. Dear heaven, she looked like a slut, with her bare breasts hanging out of the top of her dress and the skirt rucked up around her thighs. She pictured Joan's disapproving expression and shame doused the heat in her blood like cold water thrown on a fire.

'Men only want one thing,' her mother had often told Sara. *'Once you give them your body they quickly lose interest in you.'*

Sara assumed that was how her father had treated her mother. It was certainly true of Alekos. She knew about all the gorgeous blondes who had come and gone in his life, because he'd given her the task of arranging an item of jewellery from a well-known jewellers to be sent to his mistresses when he ended his affair with them. Who would choose a pretty trinket to be sent to a mistress who was also his PA? She didn't know whether to laugh or cry.

'We can't go to bed,' she told him firmly. 'You know we can't, Alekos. We shouldn't have got carried away like we did.' She watched his expression turn from puzzlement to shock at her refusal before his eyes narrowed to black slits that gleamed with anger.

'Why not?' he demanded, his clipped tone betraying his frustration. 'We are both unattached, consenting adults.'

'I work for you.'

He dismissed her argument with a careless shrug of his shoulders. 'This evening we gave the impression that we are having an affair and tomorrow's papers will doubtless carry pictures of us arriving at the art gallery together.'

'But we were only pretending to have a relationship. You don't really want me.'

'It's patently obvious how much I want you,' Alekos said sardonically. 'And you want me, Sara. Don't bother to deny it. Your body doesn't lie.'

She followed his gaze down to her bare breasts and silently cursed the hard points of her nipples that betrayed her. Red-faced, she yanked the top of her dress back into place. 'We can't,' she repeated grittily. But her resolve was tested to its limit by the feral hunger in his eyes. 'If we had an affair, what would happen when it ended?'

'I see no reason why you couldn't carry on being my PA. We work well together and I wouldn't want to lose you.'

Alekos wouldn't want to lose her as his PA, but that was all. She could not risk succumbing to her desire for him because she would find it impossible to continue to work for him after they were no longer lovers. It would be torture to know he was dating other women after he'd finished with her. And she *would* know. In the two years she had been his PA she'd learned to recognise the signs that he was having regular sex.

She felt emotionally drained from the evening. Meeting her half-siblings had made her long to be part of a family. But she certainly wasn't going to sleep with Alekos to ease the loneliness she had felt all her life. 'I think you had better leave,' she told him huskily, praying he wouldn't guess she was close to tears.

'If you really want me to go, then of course I accept your decision,' he said coldly, sounding faintly incredulous that she had actually rejected him. 'But in future I suggest you do not respond to a man so fervently if you don't intend to follow it through.'

'Are you accusing me of leading you on?' Her temper flared. 'That's a foul thing to suggest and grossly unfair. You came on to me.'

'And you hated every moment when we were kissing, I suppose?' he mocked. 'It's a little too late to play the innocent victim, Sara.'

'I'm not trying to imply that I'm a victim.' But if he knew how innocent she really was he would run a mile, she thought grimly. She suddenly remembered that they had travelled from Soho to her house in Alekos's limousine. 'If I had invited you to stay the night, what would your chauffeur have done? Would he have slept in the car?'

Alekos shrugged. 'We have an arrangement. Mike

knows to wait for a while…' He did not add anything more but Sara understood that his driver had been instructed to leave after a couple of hours if Alekos went into a woman's house and did not reappear. No doubt it was an arrangement that had been used on many occasions. Sara got on well with Mike and she would have felt so embarrassed if she'd had to face him after Alekos had spent the night with her. It brought home to her that she could not sacrifice her job, her reputation and her self-respect for a sexual liaison with her boss.

But when she followed Alekos down the hall and he opened the front door she had to fight the temptation to tell him that she had changed her mind and wanted him to stay and make love to her. Love had nothing to do with it, she reminded herself. At least not for Alekos. And she had sworn she would not make her mother's mistake and fall in love with a man who could never love her.

'Goodnight,' she bid him in a low voice.

'Sleep well,' he mocked, as if he knew her body ached with longing and regret that would make sleep impossible. As she watched him stride down the path she thought that at least she would be able to face him in the office tomorrow morning with her pride intact.

But pride was a poor bedfellow she discovered later, as she tossed and turned in her single bed. Her nipples still tingled from Alekos's ministrations and the insistent throb between her legs was a shameful reminder of how close she had come to giving in to her desire for him.

CHAPTER SIX

MONACO WAS A playground for millionaires and billion-aires, and for the last three days the tiny principality had hosted the iconic yacht show, which this year had taken place in June rather than its usual date in September. Some of the world's most impressive superyachts were moored in the harbour, the largest and most spectacular being the two-hundred-and-eighty-foot *Artemis* from leading yacht brokerage and shipyard, Gionakis Enterprises.

On Sunday morning, Alekos made his way through Port Hercules in the sunshine. Now that the show was over, the huge crowds that had packed the waterfront had gone and his route to where *Artemis* was moored was no longer blocked by yacht charter brokers, who had been keen to tour the vessel and discover the superlative luxury of her interior.

Gone too were the glamour models and hostesses who were synonymous with the prestigious show. Monaco surely boasted more beautiful women wearing minuscule bikinis that revealed their tanned, taut bodies than anywhere else in the world, Alekos thought cynically. He could have relieved his sexual frustration with any of the numerous women who had tried to catch his eye, but there was only one woman he wanted and she had studiously kept out of his way.

After the frenzy of the past three days, Alekos's preferred method to unwind had been to go for a fifteen-mile run along the coast. Now he felt relaxed as he boarded *Artemis* and walked along her deck, with nothing but the cry of gulls and the lap of water against the yacht's hull to break the silence. His sense of calm wellbeing was abruptly shattered when he entered the small saloon which he had been using as an office and found Sara sitting at a desk with her laptop open in front of her.

She was dressed in white shorts and a striped top and her hair was caught up in a ponytail with loose tendrils framing her face. Without make-up, the freckles on her nose were visible and she looked wholesome and utterly lovely. Alekos felt his gut twist.

'Why are you working already? I told you I was planning to go for a run and you could have a lie in this morning.'

'I woke early and decided to get the report about the show typed up,' she said, carefully not looking directly at him. 'I thought you wouldn't be back for another hour or so.'

'Is that why you started work at the crack of dawn, hoping to have finished the report before I came back, so that you could avoid me like you've done since you arrived on Wednesday?'

She flushed. 'I haven't avoided you. We've worked together constantly every day.'

'During the day we were surrounded by other people, and you took yourself off to bed immediately after dinner every evening. I can't believe you usually go to bed at nine p.m.,' he said drily.

The colour on her cheeks spread down her throat and Alekos wondered if the rosy blush stained her breasts. 'I was tired,' she muttered. 'The past few days have been incredibly busy.'

'I don't deny it. And because I came to Monaco a couple of days before you did, this is the first chance we have had to discuss what happened after we attended the art gallery launch last week.'

Now she did look at him, her eyes so wide and full of panic that she reminded him of a rabbit caught in car headlights. 'There's nothing to discuss. We...we got carried away, but it won't happen again.'

'Are you so sure of that?' Alekos deliberately lowered his gaze to the hard points of her nipples, outlined beneath her clingy T-shirt, and grinned when she crossed her arms over her chest and glared at him. He did not know why he took satisfaction from teasing her but he suspected it was to make him feel less bad about himself. He couldn't comprehend why he had come on to her so strong last Sunday evening. It was not his style. And she had rejected him! *Theos*—that was a first for him.

What was it about Sara that fired him up as if he were a hormone-fuelled youth instead of a jaded playboy who could take his pick of beautiful women? All week he had racked his brain for an answer while he'd been alone each night in the opulent master suite on *Artemis*, whereas at last year's show he'd enjoyed the company of two very attractive—not to mention inventive—blondes.

The only reason that made any sense—but did not make him feel good about himself, he acknowledged grimly—was simply that he wanted Sara so badly because she had turned him down. He wanted to see her sprawled on his bed, all wide-eyed and flushed with sexual heat, and he wanted to hear her beg him to make love to her because his ego couldn't deal with rejection.

She was watching him warily, and for some reason it angered him. She had been with him all the way the other night, right up until he'd suggested they go to bed. Even though she had said no, he'd sensed he could have persuaded her to change her mind. But he'd never pleaded with a woman to have sex with him before, and he had no intention of starting with his PA, who clearly had a hang-up about sex.

He leaned across the desk and tugged her arms open. Ignoring her yelp of protest, he drawled, 'It will help to make the pretence that we are lovers more convincing if you drop the outraged virgin act when your father and his guests arrive.'

Her eyes flashed with anger and she clamped her lips together as if to hold back a retort. Alekos wondered how much resistance she would offer if he attempted to probe her lips apart with his tongue. Lust swept like wildfire through him and he abruptly swung away and strode over to the door, conscious that his running shorts did not hide the evidence of his arousal.

'As you are so keen to work, you may as well type up the financial report for the shareholders. It will keep you busy until lunchtime, and as you are so averse to my company you won't want to join me for a swim in the pool, will you?' he murmured, and laughed softly at her fulminating look.

They had lunch on one of the yacht's four decks, sitting at a table set beneath a striped canopy that provided shade from the blazing Mediterranean sun. Lionel Kingsley, his son and daughter and Warren McCuskey had boarded *Artemis* at midday, and Alekos had instructed the captain to steer the yacht out of the harbour and drop anchor a couple of miles off the coast.

They were surrounded by blue, Sara thought as she looked around at the sparkling azure ocean which met a cornflower blue sky on the horizon. A gentle breeze carried the faint salt tang of the sea and lifted the voices and laughter of the people sitting around the table. She popped her last forkful of the light-as-air salmon mousse that the chef had prepared for a main course into her mouth and gave a sigh of pleasure.

After her run-in with Alekos earlier in the morning, her nerves had been on edge at the prospect of them having to act as though they were a couple. She'd fretted about the lunch, knowing that she had lied to her father about being Alekos's girlfriend and, even worse, not being truthful to Charlotte and Freddie that she was their half-sister.

But she need not have worried. Alekos had been at his most urbane and charming, although his eyes had glinted with amusement and something else that evoked a molten sensation inside her when he'd slipped his arm around her waist as they had walked along the deck to greet Lionel and his party. 'Showtime, Sara *mou*,' Alekos had murmured before he'd kissed her mouth, leaving her lips tingling and wanting more, even though she knew the kiss had been for the benefit of the interested onlookers.

Recalling that kiss now, she ran her tongue over her lips and glanced at Alekos sitting across the table from her. Heat swept through her when she discovered him watching her through narrowed eyes, and she knew that he was also remembering those few seconds when his lips had grazed hers. She tore her gaze from him when she realised that Charlotte was speaking.

'An office love affair is so romantic. When did you and Alekos realise that there was more to your relationship than you simply being his PA?'

'Um…' Sara felt her face grow warm as she struggled to think of a reply.

'It was a gradual process,' Alekos answered for her. 'Obviously, Sara and I work closely together and to begin with we were friends before our friendship developed into something deeper.'

He sounded so convincing that Sara almost believed him herself. It was true that friendship had grown between them over the last two years. But that was where fact ended and her fantasy that he would fall in love with her began, she reminded herself.

Keen to change the subject, she turned to Freddie. 'Tell me what it was like at art school. It must have been fun. I would have loved to study for an art degree.'

'Why didn't you, if it is a subject that you say you have always been interested in?'

She shrugged. 'My mother wanted me to find a job as soon as I'd finished my A levels. There was only the two of us, you see, and she struggled to pay the bills.'

'Couldn't your father have helped?'

Sara froze and was horribly aware that her father had broken off his conversation with McCuskey and was waiting tensely for her to respond to Freddie's innocent question.

'No…he…wasn't around.'

'Luckily for me, Sara joined GE,' Alekos said smoothly. 'I realised as soon as I met her that she would be an ideal person to organise my hectic life.' He rang the little bell on the table and almost instantly a steward appeared, pushing the dessert trolley. 'I see that my chef has excelled himself with a selection of desserts. My personal recommendation is the chocolate torte.'

Following his words, there was a buzz of interest around the table over the choice of dessert and the awkward moment passed. Sara gave Alekos a grateful look.

'After lunch I thought you might like to use the jet skis,' he said to Charlotte and Freddie. 'Or if you prefer an activity that involves less adrenalin there is snorkelling equipment, or the glass-bottomed dinghy is a fun way to view marine life.'

'You've got one heck of a boat here, Alekos,' McCuskey commented. 'Is it true there is a helipad somewhere on the yacht?'

'The helipad is on the bow and there is a hangar below the foredeck which is specially designed. I could give you a tour of *Artemis* if you'd like to see all of her many features.'

'I surely would,' the Texan said enthusiastically.

Sara had never had as much fun as she did that afternoon. The sea was warm to swim in and, with Charlotte and Freddie's help, she soon got the hang of snorkelling. Alekos joined them later in the day and when they took the jet skis out Sara rode pillion behind him and hung on tightly to him as they sped across the bay. With her arms wrapped around his waist and her cheek resting on his broad back, she allowed herself to daydream that it was all real—that she and Alekos were lovers and her half-siblings accepted her as their sister.

'Dad and Warren are driving back to Antibes. But

Charlotte and I are meeting up with some friends in Monte Carlo this evening,' Freddie said as they stood on deck and watched the glorious golden sunset. 'Why don't you and Alekos come with us?' He put his head on one side as he studied Sara's face. 'It's bugging me that you remind me of someone, but I can't think who.'

Alekos slid his arm around her waist. 'What do you say, *agapi mou*? Would you like to go to a nightclub?'

'Yes. But I don't mind if you'd rather not,' she said quickly, unaware of the wistful expression in her eyes.

'I want to do whatever makes you happy,' he assured her.

Sweet heaven, he was a brilliant actor, but it was all pretend, Sara reminded herself firmly. She must not allow herself to be seduced by the sultry gleam in Alekos's dark eyes and the velvet softness of his voice that made her wish for the moon even though she knew it was unreachable.

Monte Carlo at midnight was a blaze of golden lights against a backdrop of an ink-black sky. Sara followed Alekos out of a nightclub that apparently was *the* place to be seen and to see celebrities. She had spotted a famous American film star and a couple of members of a boy band, but she'd only had eyes for Alekos.

They had met up with Charlotte and Freddie's friends, and Alekos had arranged for their group to use a private booth in the nightclub. He had stayed close to her all evening, draping his arm around her shoulders when they had sat in the booth drinking cocktails, and drawing her into his arms on the dance floor so that her breasts were crushed to his chest and she was conscious of his hard thigh muscles pressed against her through the insubstantial black silk dress she had chosen to wear for a night out.

He led her over to a taxi and opened the door for her to climb inside. 'My feet are *killing* me,' she complained as she flopped onto the back seat.

Alekos slid in beside her and lifted her feet onto his lap. 'Your fault for wearing stilts for shoes,' he said, inspecting the five-inch heels on her strappy sandals. Sara caught her breath when he curled his fingers around her ankles and unfastened her shoes before sliding them off her feet. While they had been in the nightclub they had continued the pretence of being lovers in front of her half-siblings. But now it seemed way too intimate when he trailed his fingertips lightly up her calves. 'Did you enjoy yourself tonight?'

'It was the best night of my life,' she said softly. 'And the best day.' Her eyes were drawn to him. In the dark taxi his chiselled profile was shadowed and the sharp angles of his face were highlighted by the glow from the street lamps. 'Thank you for making it possible for me to spend time with Charlotte and Freddie, and with my father earlier today. I hope you weren't too bored showing Warren McCuskey around *Artemis*. I guessed you had offered to give him a tour of the yacht so that I could have time alone with Lionel.'

'Yeah, I'm all heart,' he drawled. His oddly cynical tone made Sara dart a look at him, but the taxi drew up to the jetty and he climbed out of the car. She couldn't face putting her shoes back on, and while she stood contemplating whether to walk the short distance along the jetty in bare feet Alekos scooped her up in his arms and carried her up the yacht's gangway.

'Thanks.' She silently cursed how breathless she

sounded and hoped he couldn't feel the erratic thud of her heart. 'You can put me down now.'

He continued walking into the main saloon before he lowered her down. She curled her toes into the soft carpet. Every sensory receptor on her body felt vitally alive and she was intensely aware of Alekos, of the spicy scent of his aftershave, the heat of his body and the smouldering gleam in his dark eyes. It all felt like a wonderful dream—staying on a luxurious yacht, spending time with her half-siblings and dancing the night away with a man who was so handsome it hurt her to look at him.

'I wish tonight didn't have to end.' She blurted out the words before she could stop herself and flushed, thinking how unsophisticated she sounded.

'It doesn't have to end yet. Will you join me for a nightcap?'

'Um…well, I shouldn't. It's late and we both have to be up early in the morning. You're flying to Dubai to visit Sheikh Al Mansoor, and my flight to London is at ten a.m.'

'I realise that it's three hours past your bedtime,' he said drily. 'But why not live dangerously for once?'

Alekos had simply invited her to have a drink with him. This was not a defining moment in her life, Sara told herself firmly. 'All right.' She ignored the warning in her head that sounded just like her mother's voice, and sided with the other voice that urged her to stop hiding from life and *live*. 'Just one drink.'

'Sure. You don't want to overdose on excitement.' He gave her a bland smile as he ushered her out of the main saloon and towards the stairs that led to the upper decks.

When she hesitated he murmured, 'There is champagne on ice in my suite.'

Sara had never been in the master suite before and its opulent splendour took her breath away. The décor of the sitting room and the bedroom she could see beyond it was sleek and ultra-stylish while the colour scheme of soft blue, grey and white was restful. Not that she felt relaxed. Quite the opposite as she watched Alekos slip off his jacket and throw it onto a chair before he strolled over to the bar. His white silk shirt was unbuttoned at the throat, showing his dark olive skin and a glimpse of black chest hairs. His hair fell across his brow and the dark stubble on his jaw gave him a rakish look that evoked a coiling sensation in the pit of her stomach.

The sliding glass doors were open and she stepped outside onto the private deck and took a deep breath. On this side of the yacht facing away from the port there was only dark sea and dark sky, lit by a bright white moon and stars like silver pins studding a black velvet pincushion.

Alekos's footfall was silent but she sensed he was near and turned to take the glass of pink fizz he handed her. 'Kir Royale, my favourite drink.'

'I know.' He held her gaze. 'Why were you looking sad?'

Sara sighed. 'Charlotte and Freddie both talked a lot about their happy childhoods, and how much their parents loved each other. Lionel's wife suffered from multiple sclerosis for several years and he cared for her devotedly until her death two months ago.' She bit her lip. 'If Lionel reveals that I am his daughter, all their memories of growing up in a happy family will be tainted by the knowledge that their father cheated on their mother.'

She placed her glass down on a nearby table and curled her hands around the deck rail, staring into the empty darkness beyond the boat. 'I'm afraid that my half-siblings will hate me,' she said in a low voice.

'I don't believe anyone could hate you, Sara *mou*.'

The gentleness in Alekos's voice was unexpected and it tore through her. 'I'm not *your* Sara.'

He smiled at her fierce tone. 'Aren't you?' He uncurled her fingers from the rail and turned her to face him. Sara trembled when he drew her unresisting body closer to his—so close that she could feel his heart thundering as fast as her own.

Of course she was his. The thought slipped quietly into her head. It wasn't complicated; it was really very simple. She had been his for two years and she could not fight her longing for him when he was looking at her with undisguised hunger in his eyes that made her tremble even more.

'I want you to be mine, and I think you want that too,' he murmured. She felt his lips on her hair, her brow, the tip of her nose. And then his mouth was there, so close to hers that she felt his warm breath whisper across her lips, and she couldn't deny it, couldn't deny him when it would mean denying herself of what she wanted more than anything in the world—Alekos.

Maybe it was because she had made him wait that explained the wild rush of anticipation that swept through him, Alekos brooded. And perhaps it was the lost, almost vulnerable expression on her lovely face moments ago that had elicited a peculiar tug on his heart.

The haunted look in her eyes should have warned him to back off while he still retained a little of his sanity. But it was too late. His desire for her was too strong for him to fight. Sara had driven him to the edge of reason for too long and the feel of her soft curves pressing against his whipcord body, and the little tremors that ran through her when he smoothed his hand down her back and over the taut contours of her bottom decimated his control.

He took possession of her mouth and gave a low growl of satisfaction when she parted her lips to allow his tongue access to her sweetness within. This time she would not reject him. He felt her desperation in the way she kissed him with utter abandon, and her response fuelled his urgency to feel her naked body beneath his.

He liked the little moan of protest she made when he ended the kiss and lifted his head to stare into her green eyes with their dilated pupils. She was so petite he could easily sweep her up in his arms, but he stepped back and held out his hand. 'Will you come and be mine, Sara?'

He liked that she did not hesitate. She put her fingers in his and he led her into the bedroom. His heart was pounding faster than when he'd gone for a fifteen-mile run that morning. And he was already hard—*Theos*, he was so hard; his body was taut with impatience to thrust between her slim thighs. The sight of her wearing a bikini when they had swum in the sea earlier in the day had driven him to distraction, and he had suggested using the jet skis to hide the embarrassing evidence of his arousal that his swim shorts couldn't disguise.

Most women would have played the temptress and given him artful looks as they performed a striptease for his benefit. Sara simply stood at the end of the bed and looked at him with her huge green eyes. Her faint uncertainty surprised him. She was, after all, a modern single woman in her mid-twenties and he assured himself that this could not be new for her. It was difficult to picture her as the drab sparrow who he had barely noticed in his office but, remembering the old style Sara, he thought it was likely that she hadn't had many lovers.

But he did not want her to be shy with him. He wanted her to be bold and as eager as he was. His hunger for her was so intense and he sensed that this first time would not last long. He needed her with him all the way, which meant that he must turn her on by using all his considerable skill as a lover.

'I want to see you,' he said roughly. The bedside lamps were switched off but the brilliant gleam from the moon silvered the room and gave her skin a pearlescent shimmer as he pulled the straps of her dress down, lower and lower until he had bared her breasts.

'*Eísai ómorfi.* You are beautiful,' he translated, realising he had spoken in Greek. His native tongue was the language of his blood, his passion, and he groaned as he cradled her breasts in his hands, testing their weight and exploring their firm swell before he was drawn inexorably to their dusky pink crests that jutted provocatively forwards, demanding his attention.

She shivered when he flicked his thumb pads over her nipples, back and forth before he rolled the tight nubs between his fingers until she gave a low cry that corkscrewed its way right into his gut. Giving her pleasure became his absolute focus but when he lowered his head to her breast and closed his mouth around her nipple, sucking hard, she bucked and shook and her un-

disguised enjoyment of what he was doing to her drove
him to the brink.

'Sara, I have to have you now. I can't wait,' he muttered as he straightened up and sought her lips with his,
thrusting his tongue into her mouth to tangle with hers.
Next time he would take it slow, he promised himself.
But he was fast losing control and the drumbeat of desire pounding in his veins demanded to be assuaged.

He would have liked her to undress him, maybe knelt
in front of him to pull his trousers down and then taken
him in her mouth. His body jerked at his erotic fantasy
and he swore beneath his breath. There was no time
for leisurely foreplay and he fought his way out of his
clothes with none of his usual innate grace, while she
stood watching him, her eyes widening when he stepped
out of his boxers. She stared at his rock-hard arousal,
and the way she swallowed audibly made him close his
eyes and offer a brief prayer for his sanity.

'Alekos…' she whispered.

'If you have changed your mind. Go. Now,' he gritted.

'I haven't. It's just…' She broke off and ran her fingertips lightly, almost tentatively over his proud erection.

He grabbed her hand and lifted it up to his chest
where his heart was thundering so hard he knew she
could feel it. 'Playtime's over, angel.' He tugged her
dress over her hips and it slithered to the floor. A pair
of black lacy knickers were all that hid her femininity
from him and he dealt with them with swift efficiency,
sliding them down her legs before he lifted her and laid
her on the bed.

The strip of soft brown curls between her thighs partially shielded her slick heat from his hungry gaze. He lifted her leg and hooked it over his shoulder, then did the same with her other leg, and his laughter was deep and dark when she gasped in protest.

'Beautiful,' he growled. She was splayed in front of him, open and exposed, and he had never seen anything as exquisite as he lowered his head and placed his mouth over her feminine heat.

'Oh.' She jerked her hips and clutched his hair. It crossed his mind that maybe she hadn't received pleasure this way before, and the possessive feeling that the thought elicited rang a faint alarm bell in his mind. He had never felt possessive of any woman and Sara was no different than any of the countless lovers he'd had since his first sexual experience when he was seventeen.

She squirmed beneath him. 'You can't...' She sounded scandalised, but there was something else in her guttural cry, a note of excitement that made Alekos smile.

'Oh, but I can,' he promised. And then he bent his head once more and probed his tongue into her slick heat, straight to the heart of her. Her hoarse moans filled his ears and her sweet feminine scent swamped his senses. She tasted of nectar and he licked deeper, sliding his hands beneath her bottom to angle her hips so that he could suck the tiny nub of her clitoris.

The effect was stunning. She gave a keening cry, bucking and writhing beneath him so that he gripped hold of her hips and held her fast while he used his tongue to drive her over the edge. She shattered. And watching her climax, her fingers clawing at the satin bedspread as her body shook, fired his blood and his need.

Theos, he had never *needed* a woman before. His

brother had been needy for the woman who had broken his heart, but Alekos had learned from Dimitri's death that needing someone was a weakness that made you vulnerable. Although he was loath to admit it, right now he needed Sara the same way he needed to breathe oxygen.

Somehow, Alekos retained enough of his sanity to take a protective sheath from the bedside drawer and slide it over his erection. And then he positioned himself between her spread thighs once more and his need was so fierce and consuming that the flicker of apprehension in her eyes did not register in his mind. Not until it was too late.

He could hear the sound of his ragged breaths and his blood thundering in his ears. His fingers shook as he stroked them over her moist opening and found her hot and slick and ready for him. He was so close to his goal and with a groan he thrust his way into her and froze when he felt an unmistakable resistance.

She could not be a virgin.

But the evidence was there in the sudden tension of her muscles and the way she went rigid beneath him. His brain told him to halt and withdraw, but his body was trapped in the web of his desire. A sense of urgency that was more primitive and pressing than logical thought overwhelmed him. His shock at discovering her innocence was followed by an even greater shock as he realised that he was out of control. His body was driven by a fearsome need that drove him to move inside her and push deeper into her velvet heat.

Somewhere in the crazy confusion of his mind he was aware that she had relaxed a little and she flattened her hands against his chest and slid them up to his shoulders, not pushing him away but drawing him down onto her. She shifted her hips experimentally to allow her internal muscles to accommodate him, and just that small movement blew his mind. With a sense of disbelief Alekos felt his control being stretched and stretched. Everything was happening too fast. He closed his eyes and fought against the heat surging through his veins, but he couldn't stop it… He couldn't…

He let out a savage groan as his control snapped and he came hard, his body shuddering with the force of his climax. Even as the tremors still juddered through him, shame at his lack of restraint lashed his soul. How could he have been so weak? How could Sara have made him so desperate?

And what the hell was he going to do with her now?

CHAPTER SEVEN

'WHY DIDN'T YOU tell me it was your first time?'

Alekos's voice sounded...odd, not angry exactly, but not pleased either. And perhaps his gruff tone was to be expected, Sara acknowledged. He had been anticipating a night of passion with a sexually experienced mistress, but instead he'd found himself making love to a woman whose sexual experience could be documented on the back of a postage stamp.

'It was my business,' she said huskily, finding it hard to speak past the lump that inexplicably blocked her throat.

'But now you have made it my business too.' He said something in Greek that she thought it was best she did not understand. 'I'm sorry I hurt you.' He sounded remorseful and again there was that odd tone in his voice that was not quite anger but might have been regret.

'You didn't really. I mean, just a bit at first but then it was...okay.'

'You should have told me,' he said more harshly this time.

She sighed. 'I was curious.' Not the full truth but it would do. She wanted to cry—perhaps every woman felt emotional after her first sexual experience—but she was determined to wait until she was alone before she let her tears fall.

Alekos's weight was heavy on her, pressing her into the mattress and making her feel trapped. She didn't want to look at him, but there was nowhere else *to* look when his body was still joined with hers. His dark eyes that only moments ago had blazed with desire were now chips of obsidian and his beautiful mouth was compressed into a hard line. It was impossible to believe that his lips had ever curved into a smile of sensual promise.

She pushed against his chest. 'Can we talk about this some other time, and preferably not at all? We're done, aren't we?' She bit her lip. 'To be honest, I don't understand why people make sex such a big deal.'

She could not hide the disappointment in her voice. The discomfort she'd experienced when Alekos had pushed his powerful erection into her had only lasted a few moments. The stinging sensation had faded and been replaced with a sense of fullness that had begun as pleasant, and when he'd moved, and pushed deeper, had become a tantalising throb that she had wanted to continue.

But it had ended abruptly. Alekos's ragged breaths had grown hoarser before he'd made a feral growl that sounded as if it had been ripped from his throat as he had slumped forwards and she'd felt his hot breath on her neck.

He was still on top of her. Still *inside* her. There was too much of him for her fragile emotions to cope with, and now he was frowning, his heavy brows meeting above his aquiline nose.

'No, we are not done, Sara *mou*. Nowhere near.'

'I'm not your Sara.'

He laughed softly and the rich sound curled around her aching heart. Tenderness from Alekos was something she hadn't expected and it was too beguiling for her to bear right now.

'I have indisputable proof that you are mine. Am I hurting you now?' he murmured. He shifted his position very slightly and she felt something bloom inside her, filling her once more so that her internal muscles were stretched. While she was stunned by the realisation that he was hardening again, he bent his head and captured her mouth in a slow, sensual kiss that started out as gentle and, when she responded because she couldn't help herself, became deeper and more demanding.

She was breathless by the time he trailed his lips over her cheek to her ear and nipped her lobe with just enough pressure that she shivered with pleasure that was not quite pain. He moved lower, kissing his way down her throat and over the slopes of her breasts before he flicked his tongue across one nipple and rolled the other peak between his fingers, making her gasp at the sheer intensity of the sensations he was creating.

He played her body the way a skilled musician wrung exquisite notes from an instrument, his touch now light, now masterful, and always with the utmost dedication to giving her pleasure. And all the while he moved his hips unhurriedly, sometimes in a gentle rocking motion, sometimes circling his pelvis against hers.

Each movement resulted in his erection growing harder within her and stretching her a little more, filling her until she was only aware of Alekos—the warmth of his skin, the strength of his bunched shoulder muscles beneath her hands, the power of his manhood pushing into her, pulling back, pushing into her, pulling back, in a steady rhythm that made her want more of the same.

He looked down at her and his mouth curved into a slow smile as he slid his hands beneath her bottom and encouraged her to arch her hips to accept the thrust of his body.

'Does that feel good?'

'Yes.' It felt amazing but she was suddenly shy, which was ridiculous, she told herself, when she was joined with him in the most intimate way possible.

'Tell me if it hurts.'

'It doesn't.'

'Tell me what you want.'

Oh, God, how could she tell him that his relentless rhythm was driving her mad? How could she tell him what she wanted when she didn't know? She stared up at his handsome face and thought she would die of wanting him. 'I want you to move faster,' she whispered. 'And harder. Much harder.'

'*Theos*, Sara…' He gave a rough laugh. 'Like this?' He thrust deep and, before she had time to catch her breath, he thrust again. 'Like this?'

'Yes…*yes.*'

It was unbelievable, indescribable. And so beautiful. She learned his rhythm and moved with him, meeting each thrust eagerly as he took her higher, higher. He possessed her utterly, her body and her soul, and he held her at the edge, made her wait a heartbeat before he drove into her one final time and they exploded together, her cries mingled with his hoarse groan as they shattered in the ecstasy of their simultaneous release.

Sara came down slowly. A heavy lethargy stole through her body, making her muscles relax and blocking out the hundreds of thoughts that were waiting in the wings of her mind, preparing to lambast her with recriminations. Alekos moved away from her and moments later she heard a click that she guessed was the door of the en suite bathroom closing. She wondered if it was her cue to leave. What was the protocol when you had just lost your virginity to your boss?

Oh, God, it was better not to think of that. Better not to think at all, but to keep her eyes closed and that way she could pretend it had all been a dream. Hovering on the edge of sleep, she was aware that the mattress dipped and she breathed in the elixir that was Alekos— his aftershave, sweat, the heat of his body.

In her dream she turned towards his warmth and curled up against him, her face pressed to his chest so that she felt his rough chest hairs against her cheek. In her dream he muttered words in Greek that she didn't understand as he slid his arm beneath her shoulders and pulled her close to him.

Alekos knew he was in trouble before he opened his eyes. The brush of silk on his shoulder and a faint vanilla scent were unwelcome reminders of his stupidity. Lifting his lashes, he confirmed that the situation was as bad as it could get. Not only had he had sex with Sara, but she had slept all night in his bed. *Theos*, in his *arms*.

He hardly ever spent an entire night with a lover. Sharing a bed for sleeping suggested a level of intimacy he did not want and could lead to mistaken expectations from a woman that she had a chance of being more than his mistress. Last night he had intended to leave Sara in his bed and go and sleep in another cabin.

He could not explain to himself why he had climbed

back into bed after he'd visited the bathroom. Alarm bells had rung in his head when she'd snuggled up to him, all soft and warm and dangerously tempting. He'd been tired and had closed his eyes, promising himself he would get up in a couple of minutes, and the next he'd known it was morning.

He swore beneath his breath. Sara was still asleep and he carefully eased his arm from beneath her. The sunlight filtering through the blinds played in her hair and made the silky layers burnish myriad shades of golden brown. With her English rose complexion and her lips slightly parted she looked innocent, but of course she wasn't, thanks to him, he acknowledged grimly.

What had he been thinking when he'd made love to her, not just once but twice? But that was the trouble. *He hadn't been capable of rational thought.* His actions had been driven by desire, by his need for Sara that in the crystal clarity of the-day-after-the-night-before shamed him. Discovering that she was a virgin should have immediately prompted him to stop having sex with her. But he had been unable to resist the slick, sweet heat of her body, and he'd come—*hell*, he'd come so hard. Even now, remembering the savage intensity of his release caused his traitorous body to stir.

Failing to satisfy a lover was a new experience for him and Sara's obvious disappointment had piqued his pride. He grimaced. His damnable pride was not the only reason he'd set out to seduce her a second time. He'd convinced himself it was only fair that he should gift her with the pleasure of an orgasm. Despite her inexperience, she had been a willing pupil and he'd found her ardent response to his lovemaking irresistible.

It was that thought that compelled him to slide out

of bed and move noiselessly around the bedroom while he dressed. In his mind he replayed the last conversation he'd had with his brother when he was fourteen.

'Why are you so upset just because your girlfriend cheated? You can easily find another girlfriend. Women love you.'

'No other woman could ever replace Nia in my heart,' Dimitri had said. 'When you are older you'll understand, Alekos. One day you will meet a woman who gets under your skin and you'll be unable to resist her. It's called falling in love and it's hellish.'

He wouldn't visit hell for any woman, Alekos had vowed years ago as he'd watched his brother weeping. Love had brought Dimitri to his knees. Had it also been ultimately responsible for his death? The question had haunted Alekos for twenty years.

There was no danger he would fall in love with Sara. But his weakness last night served as a warning he could not ignore. He didn't know why she had chosen to lose her virginity with him, and he did not want to know what hopes she might be harbouring about them making their pretend affair a reality.

One thing he knew for sure was that he needed to get the hell off the yacht before she woke up. A short, sharp lesson might be brutal but it was best to make it clear that all he'd felt for her was lust. He still felt, he amended when she moved in her sleep and the sheet slipped down to reveal one perfect rose-tipped breast. She was peaches and cream and he wanted to feast on her again. The strength of his desire shocked him and he strode over to the door, resisting the urge to look back at her.

Sara would probably expect to find him gone when she woke up. She knew he was planning to fly to Dubai to take part in a charity polo match organised by his friend Sheikh Al Mansoor. Kalif had brought one of his cousins to Monaco to visit the yacht show, and the three of them would fly to Dubai on the Prince's private jet. There was no reason why he should feel guilty for abandoning Sara, Alekos assured himself. After all, she was his PA and she had arranged his diary around his ten-day trip to stay at Kalif's royal palace.

Deep down, Alekos acknowledged that he was running away, and the unedifying truth did not make him feel good about himself. He was running scared, his conscience taunted him. Sara had made him lose control and it had never happened before. No woman had ever got under his skin and he hoped—*no*, he was sure—that distance would allow him to put his fascination with her into perspective. He'd responded to the chemistry between them. That was all. When he returned to the London office in ten days' time she would no doubt be as keen as him to forget about their night of passion.

Sara was woken by a *thud-thud* noise that she recognised was a helicopter's rotor blades. She opened her eyes and frowned as she looked around her. This was not her cabin on *Artemis*. This was… *Dear, sweet heaven!* Memories of the previous night flooded her mind. Last night she'd had sex with Alekos and he had not been pleased when he'd discovered it was her first time.

She turned her head on the pillow and, finding she was alone in the bed, assumed he was in the bathroom. Her thoughts flew back to last night. It had been over fairly quickly and she'd felt underwhelmed by the experience. But then Alekos had made love to her a second time, and nothing she'd ever read about sexual pleasure came close to the incredible orgasm that had exploded through her body like an electrical storm and left her shaking in its aftermath.

It had been just as good for Alekos. His harsh groan before he'd slumped on top of her had told her he'd reached his own nirvana. But what would happen now? Where did they go from here?

It suddenly seemed a good idea to get dressed before she faced him. Muscles she'd been unaware of until this morning tugged as she slid out of bed and scooped up her dress and knickers from the floor where they had scattered. The memory of his hands on her body and his mouth on her breasts and—*dear God*—between her legs when he'd bestowed a shockingly intimate caress, caused heat to bloom on her cheeks and she felt even hotter inside.

When he'd realised she was inexperienced he had tempered his passion with tenderness that had captured her heart and made her hope— *No*, she must not go down that road, she told herself firmly. Just because Alekos had made love to her with exquisite care and made her feel beautiful and desirable, she must not hope he might fall in love with her. *But he might*, whispered a little voice in her head.

The sound of rotor blades was becoming fainter, as if the helicopter was flying away. Sara frowned. Who could have been delivered to the yacht by helicopter? As far as she was aware, no guests were expected. Alekos was taking a long time in the bathroom. Struck by a sudden sense of foreboding, she knocked on the bathroom door and when he didn't answer she tried the handle and found it unlocked and the room empty. She ran over to the sliding glass doors and out onto the deck.

Looking up, she saw that it was the *Artemis* helicopter flying away from the yacht and her heart dropped faster than a stone thrown into a pool as she realised that Alekos must be on board.

She remembered she'd arranged for the pilot to fly him to the airport at Nice, and from there he would travel to Dubai. Of course she wouldn't have expected him to change his plans, but why hadn't he at least woken her to say goodbye? Because he was reluctant to face her after last night, she thought bleakly. She felt sick to think that Alekos had used her for sex. She heard her mother's voice: *'Once you've given a man what he wants you won't see him for dust.'*

Choking back a sob, Sara hurried back to her own cabin on the deck below, praying she wouldn't bump into any of the yacht's crew. She had things to do: clothes to pack, paperwork to stow in her briefcase before she was due to leave *Artemis* and travel to the airport with members of GE's sales team. Keeping busy stopped her from brooding on the fact that Alekos had abandoned her.

Laden with her suitcase and laptop, she descended to the main deck and forced a smile when she saw her father's friend Warren McCuskey walking up the gangway onto the yacht.

'I'm afraid you have just missed Alekos. He left early for an appointment.'

'Not to worry. I'll call him with the news he's been wanting to hear.' The Texan laughed. 'I've gotta hand it to your guy—he's a damned good salesman. When I met him a couple of months back I happened to say that my wife, Charlene, fancied us having a boat, and since then Gionakis hasn't missed a chance to try and persuade me to buy a yacht from GE. The day after we met at the art gallery in London he invited me to visit *Artemis* while she was in Monaco. By lucky coincidence I'd arranged to stay at Lionel's place in Antibes.'

'Did you say you had met Alekos *before* the gallery launch?' Sara strove to sound casual while her brain reminded her that Alekos did not operate on 'lucky coincidences'. He'd known Warren would be staying at her father's villa because she'd told him.

'Sure. And, like I said, he used every opportunity to use his sales tactics on me. But what really sold me on the idea of buying a yacht from his company was when he said that you are Lionel's daughter.'

Warren mopped his sunburned brow with a handkerchief and so did not notice the colour drain from Sara's face. 'Lionel is my closest friend, and if Gionakis is going to be his son-in-law I'll be happy to buy a boat from him.'

'Alekos told you that he and I are getting married?' she said faintly.

'Not in so many words. But I can tell when a fella is in love. He couldn't keep his eyes off you at lunch yesterday. I was impressed with this yacht and I've decided to buy her.'

'You want to buy *Artemis*?' Sara was stunned. The superyacht's price was two hundred million dollars, making her one of the most expensive yachts ever built. Alekos had seen a business opportunity when she'd told him that Lionel Kingsley was her father. No wonder he had suggested they could pretend to be having an affair so that she could attend functions with him and socialise with her father. He had been aware that Warren McCuskey was Lionel Kingsley's close friend; it was fairly common knowledge.

Alekos had been *so* helpful talking to Warren to give her time alone with her father, she thought cynically. She had believed his offer to help her had been genuine, out of kindness. But Alekos wasn't *kind*. He was a ruthless businessman and, unforgivably, he had betrayed her secret and told Warren that Lionel was her father.

Idiot, she thought bitterly. Why had she given herself to Alekos, knowing he was a notorious womaniser and heartbreaker? The answer—that she was in love with him—filled her with self-disgust. Did she really have so little self-worth to love a man who only loved himself?

'If you speak to Alekos, will you pass on a message?' Warren said.

'Oh, I'll give him a message, don't you worry.' She disguised her sardonic tone with a bland smile. The Texan would be shocked if he knew she intended to tell Alekos he was an arrogant, manipulative bastard. Beneath her outwardly calm exterior she was seething. Alekos had played her for a fool but she would never give him the chance to humiliate her again.

After the cloudless blue skies and golden sunshine of Monaco, the typical British summer weather of rain and a chilly wind that whipped along Piccadilly did nothing to lift Sara's spirits. It was strange to be back in the office without Alekos and she felt annoyed with herself for missing him as she tried to focus on work.

'Sara, do you have a minute?' Robert Drummond, the CEO, stopped by her desk on Friday afternoon.

'Of course. What's up, Bob?' She noticed he seemed tense. 'Can I get you a coffee?'

'No, thanks. Remind me, when will Alekos be back?'

'He's due in the office next Wednesday. His trip to

Dubai is a private visit but I can contact him if necessary.' She hadn't heard from Alekos since they had left Monaco but she had not expected to, and luckily there had been no work issues that required her to phone him.

The CEO frowned. 'Keep this to yourself. There has been some unusual trading activity of the company's shares in recent days. It's probably nothing to be concerned about but I'll keep my ear to the ground and talk to Alekos when he's back.'

After Bob had gone, Sara drummed her fingertips on her desk, wondering if she should call Alekos. She was still his PA for now and it was her job to alert him of anything that might affect the company. Her phone rang and her heart leapt into her throat when she saw his name on the caller display.

'Sara, I need you to come over immediately.' Alekos's sexy Greek accent was more pronounced than usual, making the hairs on her body stand on end. Damn the effect he had on her, she thought bitterly.

'You want me to come to Dubai?' She was pleased that she sounded cool and composed.

'I returned to London earlier than planned,' he said tersely. 'I'm working from home. I've sent Mike to collect you, so go and wait in the car park for him.'

She stared at the envelope on her desk containing her letter of resignation. The sooner she gave it to Alekos the better.

'Sara—' he sounded impatient, and nothing like the sensual lover who had spoken to her tenderly when he'd made love to her '—did you hear me?'

'Yes.' She dropped the envelope into her handbag. 'I'm on my way.'

CHAPTER EIGHT

ALEKOS'S LONDON HOME was a penthouse apartment next to the river with stunning views of the Thames, Tower Bridge and the Shard.

His valet opened the door to admit Sara into the hallway and her tension racked up a notch when she heard a female voice from the sitting room. Did he have a woman here? Maybe someone he'd met in Dubai. It was only four nights ago that he had slept with *her*. She was tempted to hand the letter in her bag to the valet and ask him to deliver it, but just then the sitting room door opened and Alekos's mother came out to the hall. When she saw Sara she burst into tears.

'No, no, Sara,' she sobbed, 'you must not allow Alekos to work. The doctor said he has to rest.'

Sara had met Lina Gionakis a few times and had found her to be charming but excitable. She frowned. 'Doctor? Is Alekos unwell?'

'He could have died,' Lina said dramatically.

'Rubbish.' Alekos's gravelly voice made Sara's pulse race as she followed his mother into the sitting room and her gaze flew to him, sprawled on a sofa by the window. He was wearing faded denim jeans, a cream shirt undone to halfway down his chest and no shoes.

She dragged her eyes from the whorls of black hairs that grew thickly on his chest and stared at his bare feet. There was something curiously intimate about seeing his feet that reminded her of when he'd stripped in front of her before he had undressed her in his bedroom on *Artemis*.

Pink-cheeked, she jerked her gaze up to his face and did a double take when she saw he was wearing a black eye patch over his right eye.

'Polo,' he said drily, answering her unspoken query. 'I was hit in the eye with a mallet during a match.'

'The doctor said you are lucky you were not blinded in your eye.' Lina wrung her hands together. 'Promise me you will wear a helmet and faceguard in future. What if you had fallen from your horse? A head injury can be fatal. Polo is such a dangerous sport and you know I couldn't bear it if I lost another son.'

'Mana, I am not a child.' Alekos was clearly struggling to control his impatience with his mother and he looked relieved when the valet returned with a tea tray. 'Sit down and Giorgos will serve you tea and cakes while I go over a few things with Sara.'

He strode out of the room and Sara followed him into his study. 'Is your eye injury serious?'

'Not really. The blow from the mallet caused a blood vessel in my eye to rupture and my vision is blocked by a pool of blood covering the iris and pupil. The condition is called a hyphema and it shouldn't result in long-term harm.' He shrugged. 'It's fairly painful and I have to use eye drops and wear the patch for a few weeks. But I'll live,' he added sardonically.

'Your mother is very upset. What did she mean when she said she couldn't bear to lose another son?'

Alekos leaned his hip against the desk and folded his arms across his chest. But, despite his casual air, Sara sensed a sudden tension in him. 'I had an older brother,' he said abruptly. 'Dimitri died…in an accident when he was twenty-one. My mother still mourns him and, as you saw just now, she is terrified of losing me or one of my sisters.'

'I'm not surprised after such a tragic event. You've never mentioned your brother to me.'

'Why would I?'

Why, indeed? she thought painfully. Alekos was an intensely private man who guarded his personal life and his family. He would not choose to confide in his PA, not even one he'd had sex with. It was a timely reminder that she meant nothing to him and she opened her handbag and gave him the letter.

'What's this?'

'My formal notice of resignation. I can't continue to work for you after we…' Colour flooded her cheeks. 'After what happened a few nights ago.'

'We had sex,' he said bluntly. 'It's too late now to be embarrassed about it.'

'But I am embarrassed. We both behaved unprofessionally and that's why I have to leave my job.'

'*Theos*, Sara.' Impatience was etched onto his hard features. 'Why are you getting so worked up because we spent one night together? It didn't mean anything.'

She felt a knife blade pierce her heart. 'You made that very clear when you left the next morning without saying a word.'

Dark colour streaked along his cheekbones. 'You were asleep.'

'*You made me feel like a whore.*' She drew a shuddering breath and would have laughed at his astonished expression if she hadn't wanted to cry. 'It would have been less insulting if you'd left a cheque for my sexual services on the pillow.'

'You wanted me as much as I desired you,' he said grimly. 'Don't pretend you were the innocent one in this.'

Alekos's words hung in the air. He must have thought she was a freak when he'd discovered she was a twenty-four-year-old virgin, she thought painfully. She had been stupidly naïve to have fallen for the well-practised seduction routine of a playboy. 'When you read the letter, you will see that I have requested to leave earlier than the three months' notice my contract stipulates. It will be easier if I go as soon as possible.'

She turned and walked over to the door, but his harsh voice made her hesitate.

'Damn it, Sara. Where's your loyalty? You can't leave me now when I need you.'

'I'm sorry about your eye, but you said there will be no long-term damage.' She fought the insidious pull on her emotions. Alekos did not need her; he simply wanted to avoid the inconvenience of having to employ another PA. 'And how dare you throw my loyalty in my face after you showed me no loyalty at all?' She breathed hard as her anger with him exploded. 'I told you that Lionel Kingsley is my father in absolute confidence. How could you betray my secret to Warren McCuskey?'

'I didn't…'

She ignored him and continued. 'You were determined to sell a yacht to Warren and you knew that Lionel has a lot of influence over him. When you learned that I was Lionel's daughter you suggested we could pretend to be a couple so I could meet my half-siblings. But the real reason was to give you access to Warren, and your manipulation worked,' she said bitterly. 'One reason why Warren has decided to buy *Artemis* is because you let him think you are in love with me—his best friend's secret daughter.'

'I didn't tell him.' Alekos's voice was as sharp as a whiplash and made Sara flinch. 'Warren asked me if I knew you were Lionel's daughter, and I said yes because it would have looked odd if you hadn't told me when we were supposedly in a relationship.'

She looked at him uncertainly. 'Then how did Warren know?'

'It's likely that Lionel confided in his closest friend.'

Sara had to acknowledge the truth of what Alekos said but it didn't ease the hurt she felt. 'You still used my relationship with my father to your advantage to promote GE.'

He did not deny it. 'There is no room for sentiment in business. Which is why I need you to carry on being my PA, for now at least.' He straightened up and walked towards her, and his face was grimmer than Sara had ever seen it.

'GE is the target of a hostile takeover bid. In the past few months a large amount of company shares have been bought, seemingly by several smaller companies. I received a tip-off that these companies are all owned by one individual who has accumulated a significant number of GE's shares. In business, an unwanted takeover bidder is known as a black knight. If the black knight acquires fifty-one per cent of GE's shares he will be able to appoint a new management team and board of directors, and effectively take over the company.'

'Do you know how close the black knight is to acquiring fifty-one per cent?'

'Too damned close. It will be more difficult for him now he's out in the open. Instead of buying up shares stealthily through his various companies, he will have to try to persuade GE's shareholders to sell stock to him.'

'Are you saying that if this black knight does manage to buy enough shares, you could lose the company that your grandfather set up?' Looking closely at Alekos, Sara saw evidence of the strain he was under in his clenched jaw and the two grooves that had appeared on either side of his mouth. Despite his cavalier treatment of her, she felt a tug on her soft heart. 'There must be something you can do to stop him.'

'There are various strategies which I am already putting in place, but my best hope—only hope, to be brutally honest—is if I can convince the shareholders, many of whom are board members, not to sell their shares and remain loyal to me.' He raked his hair off his brow. 'As you are aware, I haven't always had the support of every member of the board. In fact, the black knight is a board member.'

'Orestis Pagnotis,' Sara guessed.

'Actually, no, it's Stelios Choutos. He doesn't like the new direction I am taking GE and his takeover bid is backed by an American hedge fund. Fortunately, Warren McCuskey's decision to buy *Artemis* will win me a lot of support from shareholders. An injection of two hundred million dollars into the company's coffers couldn't have come at a better time.'

'I'm sorry about your problems, but I still intend to

resign. I don't see what use I can be.' Sara's heart jolted when Alekos moved to stand between her and the door. The patch over his eye made him look even more like a pirate and his rugged good looks were a dangerous threat to her peace of mind.

'I need to have people around me who I can rely on and trust. If you are really determined to walk away from your job for no good reason I'll allow you to leave after you've served one month's notice. The future of GE will have been decided by then,' he said grimly. 'I'll pay you a full three months' salary. But in return I will expect you to be at my call constantly while I fight to save my company.'

Sara warned herself not to be swayed by his admission that he trusted her. But didn't she owe Alekos her loyalty while GE was under threat? She bit her lip, torn between feeling it was her duty to help him and the knowledge that if she stayed in her job and saw him every day it would be harder to fall out of love with him.

'All right,' she agreed before she could change her mind. 'I'll stay on for one month. But I want six months' salary.'

The extra money would pay for the college art course she wanted to do. Instead of having to wait until she had sold her mother's house, she would be able to start the art course in the new term in September. She had never made any demands on Alekos and had put him on a pedestal, always doing her best to please him. The result was that he'd treated her badly. He had made it clear that she did not matter to him, and she realised that she had wasted two years of her life loving him when he did not deserve her love. It was time she started to value herself, Sara decided.

'I guess I shouldn't be surprised that you are as mercenary as most other women,' Alekos said in a hard voice. 'I've admitted I need your help.'

'There is no room for sentiment in business,' she quoted his words back to him coolly. 'If you want me, you're going to have to pay for me.'

Alekos felt as if his head was going to explode. His eye injury had caused him to suffer severe headaches, but he hadn't taken any of the strong painkillers he had been prescribed because they made him feel drowsy and he'd needed to have all his wits about him at a crucial meeting with a group of shareholders.

He pinched the bridge of his nose to try and control the pain in his head. Behind him, the staccato click of stiletto heels on the marble-floored foyer of GE's offices in Athens sounded as loud as gunshots. He dropped his arm as Sara came to stand beside him and saw her frown when she darted a glance at his face.

He knew he did not look his best. For the past two weeks he'd survived on patchy meals, not enough sleep and too much whisky, while he'd criss-crossed the globe to meet with shareholders and tried to persuade them to back his leadership of GE. Since Stelios Choutos had issued GE with a formal notice of an intended takeover bid the battle lines had been drawn. Shareholders either supported the company's current chairman or the disgruntled board member Stelios. So far, Stelios was winning.

Now Alekos had brought the battle to GE's birthplace in Greece. He stared at the blown-up photographs on the wall of his grandfather and founder of the company, Theo Gionakis, his father, Kostas, and brother,

Dimitri. Failure was not an option he would consider. But maybe he *was* second best, as he was certain his father had thought. He wasn't the true Gionakis heir. Self-doubt congealed in the pit of his stomach.

'Why are there photos of your grandfather, your father and your brother above the reception desk, but not a picture of you?' Sara asked.

'They are all dead,' he said bluntly. 'The photo gallery is of past chairmen. Although my brother never actually became chairman, my father had his picture placed here after Dimitri died.' Alekos's jaw clenched. 'If my brother had lived to take over from my father, maybe GE would not be under threat.'

'Surely you don't believe that?'

'I have no way of knowing whether I am as good a chairman as I have no doubt Dimitri would have been.'

He felt Sara's eyes on him but he carefully avoided her gaze. It was easier, he'd found, if he did not look directly at her. That way his heart did not thump quite so hard and he could kid himself that the effect she had on him was a temporary aberration. For the past two weeks he had spent virtually every waking hour with her while they had worked together to save the company. When he was alone in bed at night it was his fantasies about making love to her, fuelled by erotic memories, rather than worry about GE that kept him awake.

He glanced at a message on his phone. 'The helicopter is waiting for us on the helipad. Let's go.'

'Go where?' she asked as they rode the lift up to the roof of the building. 'I know you have a home in Athens, and I assumed I would check in to a hotel.'

'You will stay with me. It'll be easier if you are on the same premises when we have to work late,' he countered the argument he could see brewing in her green eyes. *Theos*, she could be stubborn. But he was damned glad she was on his team.

Sara had impressed him with her dedication to GE. She'd accompanied him on his tour of cities around Europe, as well as to the US and the Far East. They had clocked up thousands of air miles to visit GE's shareholders and at every boardroom meeting, every dinner, every long evening spent in hotel bars Sara had invariably charmed the shareholders with her warmth and grace and personable nature.

She was an asset to the company and he did not want to lose her as his PA. He dismissed the thought that he did not want to lose her at all. She was not his, and perhaps this inexplicable possessive feeling was because he had been her first lover.

They boarded the helicopter and it took off, flying over Athens and out over the coast. 'I thought we were going to your house?' Sara said.

'We are. It's down there.' Alekos pointed to a small island just off the mainland. 'I own the island. Its name is Eiríni, which means *peace* in Greek.'

The helicopter hovered above the many trees that covered the island. From the air, Eiríni appeared like an emerald jewel set amid a sapphire-blue sea and some of his tension eased. This was home, his private sanctuary, and it occurred to him that Sara was the only woman, apart from his mother and sisters, who he had ever brought here. When they landed, he pulled in deep breaths of the fresh sea air mingled with the sweet scent of the yellow mimosa bushes that lined the path leading up to the house. But, as always, the scent that filled his senses was the evocative fragrance that was Sara.

He led her from the baking sun into the cool entrance hall of the house, where they were met by his housekeeper. 'Maria will show you to your room,' he told Sara. 'Feel free to explore or use the pool and we'll meet for dinner in an hour.'

She took a small bottle of pills out of her bag and gave it to him. 'You left your painkillers on your desk back in Athens. If I were you, I'd take the necessary dose and try to rest for a while.'

Her soft voice washed over him like a mountain stream soothing his throbbing head and her gentle smile made something twist deep inside him. He wanted to lie on a bed with her and pillow his head on her breasts. But that was too needy, he thought grimly. Needing someone made you vulnerable.

'Stop fussing—you sound like my mother.'

'If I had been your mother when you were growing up, I would have sent you to your room until you'd learned some manners.'

The softness had gone from her voice and Alekos heard a note of hurt that her cool tone couldn't hide. *Theos*, what the hell was wrong with him that he couldn't even be civil? As Sara turned to follow the housekeeper he caught hold of her arm.

'I'm sorry.' He raked his hair off his brow. 'I'm under a lot of strain, but that's no excuse for me to take my bad mood out on you.'

She held his gaze, and he had a feeling she knew his secret fear that his father had been right to doubt his abilities. 'You're a good chairman, Alekos, and I believe you will win the backing of the shareholders.'

'Let's hope you're right,' he said gruffly.

* * *

When Alekos woke it was dark, and a glance at the bedside clock showed it was ten p.m. *Ten!* He jerked upright and discovered that his headache had mercifully gone. After showering, he had taken Sara's advice and swallowed a couple of painkillers before he'd stretched out on the bed for twenty minutes. That had been three hours ago. She must have thought he'd abandoned her—again.

Leaving her on *Artemis* when he'd rushed off to Dubai had not been his finest hour, he acknowledged. He had been stunned to discover she was a virgin, but what had shaken him even more was the intensity of the emotional and physical connections he'd felt with her when they had made love.

He stood up, thinking he should get dressed and go and find her. Maybe it was the painkillers that had caused his sleep to be fractured with unsettling dreams about his brother, but a more likely reason was his ever-present dread that he could lose GE, which should have been Dimitri's by birthright.

His trousers were on the chair by the window. He was about to put them on when he happened to glance at the beach. The full moon shone brightly on the sand and on Sara. Alekos frowned as he watched her walk along the shoreline. She was wearing a long floaty dress, and when a bigger wave swirled around her ankles she stumbled and fell. *Theos*, what was she doing going into the sea alone at night? He stared across the beach and his heart crashed into his ribs when he could no longer see her.

Swearing, he tore out of his room and took the stairs

two at a time. The back door was open and he ran outside and sprinted across the sand. 'Sara, *Sara*…' His breath rattled from his lungs when he saw something in the shallows. It was her dress. *'Sara?'* He ploughed through the waves. 'Where are you?'

'I'm here.' She swam out from behind some rocks and stood up and waded towards him. 'What's the matter?'

Her calm tone turned his fear to fury. *'What the hell are you doing swimming on your own in the dark?'* he bellowed as he splashed through the water and grabbed hold of her arm. 'You bloody fool. Don't you have *any* common sense?'

'Ow! Alekos, you're hurting me. Why shouldn't I swim? It's not dark—there's a full moon.' She tried to pull free of him but he tightened his grip and dragged her behind him back to the shore. She kicked water at him. 'Let go of me. You're a control freak, do you know that?'

He tugged her closer to him so that her breasts, barely covered by her wet bra, were pressed against his heaving chest. Alekos's lungs burned as if he'd run a marathon. His dream about Dimitri was jumbled in his mind with the reality of seeing Sara disappear into the sea.

'I won't have another death by drowning on my conscience.'

She stopped struggling and stared at him, her green eyes huge and dark in the moon shadow. 'What do you mean?'

He silently cursed his emotional outburst. He knew he should shrug it off and walk back to the house, but inexplicably he found he wanted to tell Sara the terrible secret that had haunted him since he was a teenager. He trusted her implicitly, but he did not want to think of the implications of that right now.

He exhaled heavily. 'My brother drowned in the sea.' Sara drew a sharp breath as he continued. 'He'd gone swimming alone at night and his body was discovered washed up on the beach the next day.'

'Oh, God, how awful. Do you know how it happened? Maybe he had an attack of cramp.'

'Dimitri was a strong swimmer and a superb athlete.' Alekos released Sara's arm and dropped down onto the sand where the waves rippled onto the beach. He loved the sea but he hated it too for taking his brother from him. He hated himself more for his failure. 'It was my fault,' he said harshly. 'I could have saved Dimitri.'

She sat down on the sand next to him. 'Do you mean you were both swimming when your brother got into trouble? I know you would have done your best to save his life,' she said softly.

He shook his head. 'I wasn't with him. At the inquest his death was recorded as an accident. But...' he swallowed hard '...I believe Dimitri took his own life.'

Again she inhaled sharply. 'Why do you think that?'

'Because he told me he wanted to die. My brother was heartbroken when he found out his girlfriend had cheated on him, and he said to me that he didn't want to live without her.' Alekos raked his hair off his brow with an unsteady hand as his mind flew back to the past. Aged fourteen, he hadn't understood why Dimitri had cared so deeply for a woman.

'You'll understand when you fall in love,' Dimitri had told him. *'You'll find out how love catches you when you least expect it and eats away at you until you can't*

*think or sleep or eat for thinking about the woman you
love. And when you find out that she doesn't love you,
love destroys you.'*

Alekos had vowed when he was a teenager that love
would never have a chance to destroy him like it had
Dimitri. But for twenty years he'd felt guilty that he had
not taken his brother's threat to end his life seriously
and he hadn't sought help for Dimitri. His parents had
been devastated by their oldest son's death and Alekos
hadn't wanted to add to their grief by revealing that he
believed Dimitri had committed suicide.

'I had spoken to my brother earlier on the day that
he died, and he told me he felt like walking into the sea
and never coming back. But I didn't take him seriously.
I assumed he'd get over Nia and go back to being the
fun, happy guy my brother was—until he fell in love.'

Alekos's jaw clenched. 'Love destroyed him, and
I did nothing to save him.' He tensed when Sara put
her hand on his arm. Her fingers were pale against his
darkly tanned skin. She did not say anything but he
sensed compassion in her silence and it helped to ease
the raw feeling inside him.

'My memories are of him laughing, always laughing,' he said thickly. 'But on that day I found him crying. I was shocked but I still didn't do anything. I should
have told my parents that Dimitri had suicidal thoughts.
I didn't understand how my amazing brother, who everyone loved, could really mean to throw away his life
and hurt his family over a goddamned love affair.'

'I don't believe you could have done anything, if your
brother was determined to take his life,' Sara said gently. 'He may have had other problems you didn't know
about. Young men in particular often find it hard to talk

about things. But you don't know for certain that he did commit suicide. Presumably he didn't leave a note as the inquest recorded an accidental death.'

'He told me what he intended to do but I've never confided to anyone what I'm convinced was the real reason for Dimitri's death.'

'And so you have kept your guilt a secret for years, even though you don't know for sure that you have anything to feel guilty about. Dimitri's death *could* have been an accident. But even if it wasn't, you were in no way to blame, Alekos. You were young, and you were not responsible for your brother.'

Sara stood up. 'We should go back to the house. It must be late, and there is another meeting with shareholders tomorrow.' She brushed sand from her legs. 'I'm going for a quick swim to wash off the sand but I'll stay close to the shore.'

'I'll come with you.' He jumped up and followed her into the sea. The water was warm and its silken glide over his skin cleansed his body and his mind. The fact that Sara had not judged him and had tried to defend him helped him to view the past more rationally. *Could* it simply have been a terrible coincidence that Dimitri had died soon after confiding that he was depressed? Alekos had never considered the possibility before because he'd blamed himself when he was fourteen and he'd carried on blaming himself without questioning it.

He swam across the bay and back again, once, twice, he lost count of how many times as he sought to exorcise his demons, cutting through the water with powerful strokes until finally he was out of breath.

He watched Sara wading back to the beach. Her impromptu swim meant that she was in her underwear and her wet knickers were almost see-through so that he could make out the pale globes of her buttocks. When she turned to look for him, he saw in the moonlight her dark pink nipples through her wet, transparent bra.

Desire coiled through him, hardening him instantly so that he was glad he was standing waist-deep in the water. But he couldn't remain in the sea all night. He knew from her stifled gasp that she had noticed the bulge beneath his wet boxer shorts when he walked towards her. As he drew closer to her he watched her pupils dilate until they were dark pools, full of mystery and promise, and he asked the question that had been bugging him since the night they had spent together.

'Why did you choose me to be your first lover?'

CHAPTER NINE

SARA KNEW THAT telling Alekos the truth was not an option. Even if she was brave enough, or foolish enough, to admit she loved him, the revelation was not something he would want to hear. She understood him better now that he had told her about the nature of his brother's death. Living with the belief that Dimitri had taken his own life because of a failed love affair explained a lot about Alekos's opinion of love.

'Love is simply a sanitized word for lust,' he'd once sneered. The truth was that he blamed love for his brother's death as much as he blamed himself for not preventing Dimitri's suicide—if it *had* been suicide.

She frowned as she examined her own past that, like Alekos, she had allowed to influence her for far too long.

'I grew up being told by my mother that men only want women for one thing. Mum never revealed who my father was but she made it clear that she blamed him for abandoning her when she fell pregnant with me.'

She paused, remembering the brittle woman who she had called Mum and yet she'd never felt any kind of bond between them. Her mother's unplanned pregnancy had resulted in an unwanted child, Sara thought painfully. When she'd been old enough to start dating she had never allowed things to go too far, and when guys had dropped her because she refused to sleep with them it had reinforced her mother's warning that men only wanted sex. 'I'm sure she had loved my father and I think she continued to love him up until her death. I'm certain she never had another relationship after Lionel went back to his wife.'

She stirred the wet sand with her toes. Alekos was standing very close and she was agonisingly aware of him. The moonlight slanted over his broad shoulders and made the droplets of water clinging to his chest hairs sparkle. 'When I finally met my father I realised that he wasn't a bad person. He admitted he'd made a mistake when he'd had an affair with my mother. But she'd known he was married and so it was her mistake too.'

Sara made herself look directly at Alekos. He still had to wear the eye patch and, with a day's growth of dark stubble covering his jaw, he looked more like a pirate than ever. Dark, dangerous and devastatingly attractive. 'I had sex with you because I wanted to. You didn't coerce me or pretend that it meant anything to you—and that's fine because it didn't mean anything to me either.'

'But why me?' he persisted. 'Why not Paul Eddis, for instance? You seemed pretty friendly with him at the board members' dinner.'

She shrugged. 'Paul is a nice guy, but there was no spark between us like there was between you and me.'

'Was?' Alekos said softly. 'I would not use the past tense.' He curved his arm around her waist and tugged her into the heat of his body. The effect on her was elec-

trifying and she was mortified, knowing he must feel the hard points of her nipples. Her brain urged her to step away from him but her body had other ideas and she was trapped by her longing for him when he lowered his head towards her.

'Is this the spark you referred to?' he growled. He kept her clamped against him while he ran his other hand down her spine and lower, sliding his fingers beneath the waistband of her knickers to caress her bare bottom. 'Sexual chemistry enslaves both of us, Sara *mou*.'

She couldn't deny it, not when her body shook, betraying her need for him as he covered her mouth with his and kissed her deeply, hungrily, making the spark ignite and burn. He'd called it *chemistry* and she told herself that was all it was. His story about his brother had touched her heart, but it had also shown her that Alekos would not fall in love with her because he despised love and maybe he was afraid of it.

She could end this now. But why deny herself what she so desperately wanted? Alekos was an incredible lover. True, she had no one to compare him to, but instinctively she knew that when they'd made love it had been magical for him too. She had already decided to leave her job and she had two weeks left to serve of the month's notice period they had agreed on.

Why shouldn't she make the most of the time she had with him and then walk away with her head held high? Her mother had spent her life loving a man she couldn't have. There was no way she was going to do the same, Sara vowed. Knowing that Alekos would never love her freed her from hope and expectation and allowed her to simply enjoy his skill as a wonderful lover.

And so she kissed him back with a fervour that revealed her desire and made him groan into her mouth when she traced her fingertips over his chest and abdomen, following the arrow of black hairs down to where his wet boxer shorts moulded the burgeoning length of his arousal.

His hands were equally busy as he unfastened her bra and peeled the sodden cups away from her breasts so that he could cradle their weight in his palms. 'Beautiful,' he muttered before he bent his head and took one nipple into his mouth, sucked hard until she cried out, and her cry echoed over the empty beach. Then he transferred his lips to her other nipple and flicked his tongue across the tender peak while simultaneously he slid his hand into the front of her knickers and pushed his finger into her molten heat.

Her legs buckled and he tightened his arm around her waist and lowered her onto the sand, coming down on top of her so that his body covered hers. She was aware of him tugging her panties off and her excitement grew when he jerked his boxers down and his erection pushed into her belly. His ragged breaths filled her ears and his male scent swamped her senses. She licked his shoulder and tasted sea salt.

'Open your legs,' he said hoarsely.

She wanted to feel his length inside her and she shared his impatience. But his voice broke through the sexual haze clouding her brain and she remembered something vital.

'We can't here. I'm not on the pill.' Not even her overwhelming desire for Alekos was worth risking an unplanned pregnancy.

He tensed and swore softly as he lifted himself off

her and pulled up his boxers before he held out his hand and drew her to her feet. 'I can't go back to the house naked,' she muttered as he began to lead her up the beach. 'One of the staff might see me.'

'None of them sleep here. There is a small fishing village on the island and all the staff return to their own homes every evening.' He scooped her up in his arms and strode across the sand. 'So, are you going to sleep with me, Sara *mou*?' His sensual smile did not disguise the serious tone of his voice.

'I hope not.' She grinned when he frowned. 'I'll be very disappointed if all we do is sleep.'

Laughter rumbled in his big chest. 'Do you know the punishment for being a tease?' He proceeded to tell her exactly how he intended to punish her, so that by the time he carried her into his bedroom and laid her on the bed Sara was shivering with anticipation and a wild hunger that grew fiercer when he slid a protective sheath over his erection and positioned himself between her thighs.

He drove into her with a powerful thrust that made her catch her breath as she discovered again his size and strength. He filled her, fitted her so perfectly as if he had been designed exclusively for her. She pushed away the dangerous thought and concentrated on learning every inch of his body, running her hands over his chest and shoulders, his long spine and smooth buttocks that rose and fell in a steady rhythm.

She arched her hips to meet each thrust as he plunged deeper, harder, faster, taking her higher with every measured stroke. He was her joy and her delight, her master and tutor. Her love.

Terrified she might say the words out loud, she

cupped his face between her hands and kissed his mouth.

'Ah, Sara.' His voice sounded oddly shaken, as if he too felt a connection between them that was more than simply the joining of their mouths and bodies. Don't look for things that are not there, Sara told herself. Enjoy this for what it is—fantastic sex.

Alekos showed her how fantastic, how unbelievably amazing sex could be when he slid his hands beneath her bottom and lifted her hips to meet his devastatingly powerful thrust that hurtled her over the edge and into ecstasy. It was beyond beautiful, and she sobbed his name as pulses of pleasure radiated out from deep in her pelvis. The fierce spasms of her orgasm kept shuddering through her while he continued to move inside her. His pace was urgent now as he neared his own release. And when he came, it was with a groan torn from his throat as his body shook so hard that she wrapped her arms around him and held him tight against her heart.

Another week passed, as tense and turbulent as the weeks preceding it, as Alekos fought to save the business his father had entrusted to him. In many ways it was the worst time of his life. Endless meetings with shareholders at GE's offices in Athens, strategy meetings with his management team and, hanging over him, the possibility he refused to consider—that he might fail. It *should* have been the worst time of his life and the fact that he could smile—*Theos,* that he could actually be happy—was totally down to Sara.

At work she was a calming presence, offering thoughtful and intelligent suggestions when he asked her advice—which he had found himself doing more and more often. She charmed the shareholders and the board members liked and trusted her. Sara was an asset in the office as his PA, and when they returned to Eiríni each evening she delighted him in her role as his mistress.

Often they walked down to the village and sat on the small harbour to watch the fishing boats unload the day's catch. Later they would return to the house and eat dinner served on the terrace by his housekeeper before they went to bed and made love for hours until exhaustion finally claimed them. Alekos was waiting to grow bored of Sara, but when he woke each morning and studied her lovely face on the pillow beside him he felt an indefinable tug in his chest and a rather more predictable tug of sexual hunger in his groin that he assuaged when he woke her and she was instantly aroused and ready for him.

'Why do you think your father would blame you for GE's problems when you yourself told me that hostile takeover bids are a common threat to businesses?' she asked him one day, after he'd confided that he felt he had let his father's memory down.

'He doubted my ability to run the company as successfully as he believed Dimitri would have done.' Alekos rubbed a towel over his chest after he'd swum in the pool. He sat down on a lounger next to where Sara was sunbathing in a tiny green bikini which his fingers itched to remove from her shapely body that drove him to distraction.

It was Sunday, and after six crazily busy days of working he had decreed that today they would not leave the island. In truth, he would have been happy not to leave the bedroom they now shared, but Sara had murmured that they couldn't spend *all* day having sex.

'Why do you think your father compared you to your brother?'

He shrugged. 'Dimitri was the firstborn son and my father groomed him for his future role as chairman of GE from when he was a young boy. My relationship with my father was much more distant. I was the youngest of his five children, the second son. When Dimitri died and I became my father's heir he made it obvious that I was second best. Sometimes,' he said slowly, 'I wondered if he wished that I had died and Dimitri had lived.'

Sara sat up and faced him, her green eyes bright and fierce. 'I'm sure that's not true. It must have been a difficult time for all the family, but particularly for your parents who were grieving for their son. It sounds like he was very popular.'

'Everyone loved Dimitri.'

'Especially you. I think you were very close to your brother,' she said softly.

'I idolised him.' Images flashed into Alekos's mind: Dimitri teaching him to sail, the two of them kicking a football around the garden, that time when he'd accidentally smashed the glass panes of the greenhouse with a misaimed kick and his brother had taken the blame. He had blocked out his memories of Dimitri because when he'd been fourteen it had hurt too much to think about him. It still hurt twenty years later. And he was still angry. If his brother hadn't fallen in love with some stupid girl he would still be here, still laughing, still Alekos's best friend.

He hadn't spoken about Dimitri in all those years

and he did not understand why he had told Sara things that he'd buried deep inside him. He didn't want her compassion, he didn't want to want her so badly that he found himself thinking about her all the time. His crazy obsession with her would pass, he assured himself. Desire never lasted and the more often he had sex with her, the quicker he would become sated with her and then he could move on with his life and forget about her.

He walked back over to the pool and dived in, swimming length after length while he brought his emotions under control. Of course he did not need Sara. She was simply a pleasant diversion from his work problems.

She came to sit at the edge of the pool and he swam up to her. 'How about we have some lunch, followed by an afternoon siesta?'

'Hmm...' She appeared to consider his suggestion. 'Or we could forget lunch and just go for a lie-down.'

'Aren't you hungry?'

'I'm very hungry.' Her impish smile made his gut twist and he pulled her into the water, ignoring her yelp that the water was cold.

He felt angry with himself for his weakness and angry with her for making him weak. 'In that case I'd better satisfy your appetite, hadn't I,' he mocked as he untied the strings of her bikini top and pulled it off, cupping her breasts in his hands and playing with her nipples until she moaned softly.

He was completely in control, and he proved it when he carried her up to the bedroom and placed her face down onto the bed. He made love to her using all his considerable skill until she climaxed once, and when she came down he took her up again and only when she buried her face in the pillows to muffle her cries as she had a second orgasm did he finally let go, and felt the drenching pleasure of his own release.

By the middle of their second week in Greece the situation with GE started to look more hopeful, as increasing numbers of shareholders pledged their alliance to Alekos and refused to sell their shares in the company to Stelios Choutos. Alekos was still tense and Sara knew he would not be able to relax while GE and his position as chairman were still threatened. But, although she continued to be supportive, she had a niggling worry of her own that made her pop to the chemist during her lunch break. Of course, having bought a pregnancy test, she felt the symptoms that her period was about to start and, although the dull pain low in her stomach was annoying, she felt relieved that she wouldn't need to use the test.

The news came on Friday afternoon. Alekos strode into Sara's office, which adjoined his, and found her standing by the window, gazing up at the iconic Acropolis. She pulled her mind from her thoughts and her heart leapt when she saw the grin on his face.

'We won.' He swept her into his arms. 'Stelios's financial backers have pulled out and I've just had a call confirming he has withdrawn his takeover bid.'

'So it's over? The company is safe and you will continue to be chairman?' She blocked out the realisation that the end of the battle for GE meant that her affair with Alekos would also be over.

'I have the unanimous backing of the board, including Orestis Pagnotis.'

His victory made him almost boyish and he swung her round before claiming her lips in a fierce kiss that deepened to a slow and achingly sweet exploration of her mouth with his tongue. Sara was trembling when he finally released her and she moved away from him while she struggled to regain her composure.

'Congratulations. I never doubted you.'

'I know.' He no longer needed to wear the eye patch now that his injury was completely healed, and his eyes gleamed as he held her gaze. 'Your support was invaluable. We work well together as a team. We'll fly to back to London tomorrow and start focusing on what GE is renowned for, which is to make the best yachts in the world.'

Sara did not say anything then, but when the helicopter flew them to the island and they walked up to the house Alekos slipped his hand into hers. 'You're very quiet.'

'I was thinking that this is our last night on Eiríni—and our last night together. Today was the final day of my notice period,' she reminded him when he frowned. 'I've arranged for a temporary PA to fill my place while you hold interviews and appoint a permanent member of staff.'

He looked shocked, and that surprised her until she told herself he'd been too busy fighting for his company to have been aware that her notice period had finished. She followed him into the sitting room and looked through the glass doors that opened onto the garden where the swimming pool was a brilliant turquoise beneath a cloudless blue sky. She had fallen in love with Alekos's island and it would have a special place in her heart for ever.

Alekos crossed to the bar and poured them both a drink, as he did every evening: a crisp white wine for her and a single malt Scotch with ice for him. Usually they carried their drinks out to the terrace, but this evening he drained his glass in a couple of gulps and poured himself another whisky.

'You could stay on,' he said gruffly. 'Why do you want to leave? I know you enjoy your job.'

'I do enjoy it, but actually I never wanted to be a secretary. I only did it because I needed to help my mother pay the mortgage. Now I'm selling the house and I have plans to do something different with my life.'

'I see.' Alekos did not try to persuade her to stay, nor did he ask about her future plans, Sara noted. She ignored the pang her heart gave and reminded herself that it was time she took control of her life. 'We both know that our affair…or whatever it is we've been having for the past few weeks…was temporary. I think it will be better to end our professional and personal association once we are back in London.'

Once again a flicker of surprise crossed his sculpted features. She was possibly the only woman who had ended a relationship with Alekos before he was ready for it to finish, Sara thought wryly. It was only the thought of her mother's empty life that kept her strong when her treacherous heart and traitorous body both implored her to be his mistress for as long as he wanted her.

'In that case we had better make the most of tonight,' he said in a cool voice that forced her to acknowledge that she really did mean nothing to him other than as a good PA and a good lay. Knowing it helped her to harden her heart when he drew her into his arms and kissed her with such aching tenderness that she could almost believe he was trying to persuade her to change her mind.

It was just great sex, she reminded herself as he undid the buttons on her blouse and slid his hand into her bra to caress her breast. He stripped her right there in the sitting room and shrugged out of his clothes, taking a condom from his trouser pocket before he pushed her back against the sofa cushions. He hooked her legs over his shoulders so that she was splayed open to him and used his tongue to such great effect that she gasped his name when he reared over her and thrust into her so hard that she came instantly.

It was the beginning of a sensual feast that lasted long into the night and Alekos's passion and his dedication to giving her pleasure tested Sara's resolve to leave him to its limits. She wished the night could last for ever, but with the pale light of dawn came a reality that stunned her.

She woke to the sound of the shower from his bathroom and the horrible lurch her stomach gave sent her running into her own bathroom. There could be a number of explanations of why she had been sick, but although she still had an uncomfortable cramping pain in her stomach her period was now over a week late. The pregnancy test took mere minutes to perform and the wait for the result seemed to last a lifetime.

Alekos knocked on the door while she was still clinging to the edge of the basin because her legs had turned to jelly. 'I'll meet you downstairs for breakfast.'

'Sure.' She was amazed that her voice sounded normal. 'See you in a minute.' She almost threw up again at the thought of food, and the much worse prospect of telling Alekos her news. But not telling him was not an option. She wasn't going to make *every* mistake her mother had made, Sara thought grimly.

He found her on the beach, standing on the wet sand where the waves rippled over her bare toes. Alekos remembered how he had seen Sara walk into the sea the night they had arrived on the island, and his body tightened at the memory of how she had come apart in his arms. Sex with her was better than he'd known with any other woman but, *Theos*, he wasn't going to beg her to stay with him. The idea of him pleading with a mistress was laughable but he didn't feel in the mood to laugh, even though he had won the battle to keep GE. Curiously, he hadn't given a thought to the company since Sara had announced her intention to leave him when they went back to London.

'Don't you want something to eat?' he said as he walked up to her. 'The helicopter will be here to collect us in a few minutes.'

'I'm not hungry.'

She was pale and he frowned when he saw her mouth tremble before she firmed her lips. The breeze stirred her hair and Alekos smelled the evocative scent of vanilla. 'What…?' he began, unable to rationalise his sudden sense of foreboding.

'I'm pregnant.'

She said the words in a rush, as if they might have less impact. But they left him reeling. He stared at her slender figure, which of course showed no signs yet that a new life was developing inside her. Was it possible she was expecting his baby? He had never thought about fatherhood, apart from in a vague way as an event that he supposed would happen at some point in his future. His family impressed on him the need for him to provide an heir. But this was real. If Sara was telling him the truth, and he had no reason to doubt her, he was going to be a father and he couldn't begin to assimilate the emotions churning inside him. Crazy though it was, he felt a flicker of excitement at the idea of holding his child in his arms. *Theos*, he hoped he would be a good father.

In the years since his brother had died Alekos had become adept at hiding his feelings and his coolly logical brain took charge. 'You're sure?'

'I did a test this morning and it…it was positive. My period is a week late, but I thought…' she bit her lip '… I hoped there was another explanation. We've always been careful.'

Alekos went cold as he recalled that he had been careless that first time when they had been on *Artemis*. His hunger for Sara had been so acute that he'd made love to her a second time immediately after they'd had sex.

He stared out across the sea—flat and calm today, it looked like a huge mirror reflecting the blue sky above, but the idyllic scene did not soothe his tumultuous thoughts. His irresponsible behaviour had resulted in Sara conceiving his child and the implications were huge. He should have taken more care. He should have fought his weakness for Sara. Anger with himself made his voice clipped and cold.

'In that case a damage limitation strategy is necessary.'

She frowned. 'What do you mean by damage limitation?'

'How do you think GE's board members will react to the news that I have fathered an illegitimate child?'

he said grimly. 'Once the press get hold of the story—as they undoubtedly will—I'll be accused of being an irresponsible playboy and that kind of reputation will not go down well with the board or the shareholders, especially now, so soon after the hostile takeover bid. There is only one solution. We will have to get married.'

He looked at her stunned expression and ignored the inexplicable urge to enfold her in his arms and promise her that everything would be all right. Instead he drawled, 'Congratulations, Sara *mou*. You've done what many other women dream of and secured yourself a rich husband.'

She flinched as if he had struck her, but then her chin came up. 'Firstly, I have never been *yours*, and secondly I am not any other woman—I'm me, and I would never marry for money. Your arrogance is astounding. I'm certainly not going to marry you to save your reputation.'

Sara spun round and walked up the beach towards the house. She heard the helicopter overhead and felt glad that soon she would be on it and leaving Eiríni. She wished she could leave Alekos behind. She hadn't expected him to be pleased about her pregnancy. Pleased had not been *her* first reaction when she'd stared at the blue line on the pregnancy test that confirmed a positive result. She felt stunned and scared and very alone, and Alekos's implication that she was a gold-digger who had somehow engineered falling pregnant to snare him was so unfair that tears choked her.

'Would you deny the child its father then, Sara?'

She stopped walking and turned to find he was right behind her, so close that she breathed in his aftershave, mingled with an indefinable scent that was uniquely Alekos. 'You don't want a child,' she muttered.

'It doesn't matter what I want or don't want. The child is my heir and if we marry he or she will inherit not only GE but the Gionakis fortune. If you refuse to marry me I will financially support my child, but in the future I will take a wife and any legitimate children born within the marriage will bear my name and be entitled to inherit my legacy.'

Alekos trapped her gaze with his eyes that were as black and hard as pieces of jet. 'Will you deny your child its birthright the way you were denied yours, Sara? You told me you wish you'd grown up knowing your father. Can you really deprive your child of the chance to grow up with both its parents?'

CHAPTER TEN

ALEKOS HAD HIT her with an emotional body blow. He had aimed his argument straight at her heart, aware that she would do anything to give her baby a father—even if it meant she had to marry him.

She had tried to dissuade him. During the helicopter flight from the island and when they'd boarded his private jet bound for London, she had offered various suggestions of how they could both have a role in their child's life. But his response had been unequivocal. They must marry before the baby was born so that it was legitimate.

She looked across the plane to where he was sitting in one of the plush leather armchairs and her heart predictably gave a jolt when she found him watching her. He was casually dressed in grey trousers and a white shirt open at the throat, showing his tanned skin that had turned a darker shade of olive-gold from two weeks in the hot Greek sun. His hair was longer, and the black stubble on his jaw reminded her of the faint abrasion marks on her breasts where his cheek had scraped her skin when he'd made love to her numerous times the previous night.

Their last night together, she had believed. Now she

wondered if he intended their marriage to include sex, and if—or perhaps that should be when—he tired of her would he have discreet affairs that did not attract the attention of the press or the board members?

'I will make a press statement on Monday announcing our engagement and forthcoming marriage.'

Sara's stomach lurched. 'Why so soon? We should at least wait until I've seen my doctor to confirm my pregnancy. The test showed that I am about five weeks, and I believe a first scan to determine when the baby is due is at around eight to ten weeks.'

'I can't risk the media finding out you are pregnant before I've put an engagement ring on your finger. The board members are jittery after the takeover bid. The news that I am going to marry my sensible secretary and leave my playboy days behind will bolster their confidence in me. For that reason I've made an appointment for us at a jewellers so that you can choose a ring.'

Everything was happening too fast, she thought frantically. Yesterday she'd believed she would never see Alekos again after they had returned to England, but now she was expecting his child and he was bulldozing her into marriage.

'I don't believe a loveless marriage will be good for anyone, including the baby.' She imagined a future where Alekos had mistresses and she became bitter like her mother, and said rather desperately, 'It can't possibly work.'

'My parents did not marry for love and had a very successful marriage.' Alekos opened his laptop, signalling that the conversation was over. It was convenient for him to marry her to keep GE's board members happy, Sara thought. And by becoming his wife she would be doing the best thing for the baby. But what about what was best for her? How could she marry Alekos when she loved him but he would never love her? But how could she deny her baby the Gionakis name? The stark answer was that she couldn't.

The jewellers was in Bond Street and the price tags on the engagement rings made Sara catch her breath. 'Choose whichever ring you want,' Alekos told her. 'I don't care how much it costs.'

But diamond solitaires the size of a rock were not her style, and she finally chose an oval-shaped emerald surrounded by white diamonds because Alekos commented that the emerald matched the colour of her eyes.

'I thought you were taking me home,' she said when the limousine drew up outside his apartment block.

'This will be your home from now on. I'll have your clothes and other belongings packed up and sent over from your house. But I want you here, where I can keep an eye on you.'

She looked at him suspiciously. 'You make it sound like I'm your prisoner. Are you worried I'll leak the story to the press that I am expecting the chairman of GE's baby?'

'*No*. You proved your loyalty to me and to the company when you helped me fight off the hostile takeover.' Alekos raked his hair off his brow and she was surprised to see colour flare on his cheekbones. 'I want you to stay with me because you are pregnant and you need looking after.'

'Of course I don't.' She tried to ignore the tug on her heart at the idea of him taking care of her as if she were a fragile creature instead of a healthy, independent woman.

'You're pale, and you fell asleep on the plane and in the car just now,' he persisted.

'I'm tired because I didn't get much sleep last night.' She blushed as memories of the many inventive ways he had made love to her for hours the previous night flooded her mind. The gleam in his eyes told her he was remembering their wild passion too. 'Alekos…?'

'Yes, it will be a real marriage in every way,' he drawled.

Her face burned. 'How did you know I was going to ask that?'

'Your eyes are very expressive and they reveal your secrets.'

Sara prayed they didn't, but she carefully did not look at him when he showed her to a guest room in his penthouse because she didn't want him to guess she was disappointed that she would not be sharing his bed until they were married.

The following week passed in a blur. News of their engagement was mentioned in most of the newspapers and Sara was glad to hide away in the penthouse to avoid the paparazzi, who were desperate to interview the woman who had tamed the notorious Greek playboy Alekos Gionakis.

Her father phoned to offer his congratulations, but when she asked him if he would attend her wedding with her half-siblings Lionel hesitated for so long that Sara's heart sank.

'Why don't you tell Charlotte and Freddie Kingsley you are their sister?' Alekos asked when he discovered her in tears. He had come home from the office unexpectedly in the afternoon and found her lying on the sofa.

She shook her head. 'I can't betray my father to his children. Perhaps it will be better if he never tells them about me and they won't know that he was once unfaithful to their mother.'

Alekos sat down on the edge of the sofa and studied her face intently. 'You're as white as a sheet. How many times have you been sick today?'

'Three or four.' She tried to shrug off his concern. 'Nausea and tiredness are normal in early pregnancy and I'll probably feel better soon.'

But she didn't. Over the next few days the sickness became more frequent and the dull ache on the right side of her abdomen that she'd had on and off for weeks turned into a stabbing pain. Sara had read that a miscarriage was fairly common in the first three months of pregnancy and nothing could be done to prevent nature taking its course.

For the first time since the shock of finding out that she was pregnant her baby became real in her mind. She pictured a little boy with black hair and dark eyes like his daddy and she felt an overwhelming sense of protectiveness for the new life inside her. 'Hang on, little one,' she whispered when she went to bed early that night, praying that if she rested her baby would make it through the crucial early weeks of her pregnancy.

The pain woke her some hours later. A sensation like a red-hot poker scourging her insides was so agonising that she struggled to breathe. Sadness swept through her as she realised that she was probably going to lose the baby and when she fumbled to switch on the bedside light the sight of blood on the sheets confirmed the worst. But the amount of blood shocked her and the pain in her stomach was excruciating. She felt faint, and her instincts told her something was seriously wrong.

'Alekos...' Dear God, what if he couldn't hear her and she bled to death, alone and terrified? She called on every last bit of her fading strength. '*Alekos*...help me...'

'Sara?' She heard the bedroom door open and the overhead light suddenly illuminated the room. She heard Alekos swear and she heard fear in his voice. 'I'm calling an ambulance.' His hand felt cool on her feverish brow. She tried to speak but she felt so weak. His face swam in front of her eyes as he leaned over her. 'Hang on, Sara *mou*,' he said hoarsely, repeating the plea she had made to her baby. But pain was tearing her apart and she slipped into blackness.

Someone, at some time—Alekos did not know who or when—had come up with the gem of wisdom, *You don't know what you've got till it's gone*. The quote had been painfully apt while he had paced up and down the waiting room while Sara had undergone emergency surgery to stop serious internal bleeding resulting from an ectopic pregnancy.

'An ectopic is when a fertilised egg implants in a fallopian tube instead of in the womb,' the obstetrician at the hospital where Sara had been rushed to by ambulance had explained to Alekos. 'The pregnancy cannot continue but the condition is not life-threatening unless the tube ruptures, which unfortunately occurred in Miss Lovejoy's case.'

An hour-long operation and two blood transfusions later, Sara was transferred to the intensive care ward and a nurse told Alekos she had been lucky to survive.

He'd known that, even without much medical knowledge. The sight of her lying pale and lifeless on the blood-soaked sheets was something he would never forget.

It had been much later, when he'd sat by her bed in ITU, steadfastly refusing the nurse's suggestion to go home and get some sleep, when he'd allowed himself to think about the baby they had lost, and the fact that he had very nearly lost Sara. He had spent his life since he was fourteen building a fortress around his heart so that nothing could hurt him like Dimitri's death had. So why were his eyes wet, and why did it feel as if a boulder had lodged in his throat making swallowing painful?

Five days later, he stepped into her room in the private wing of the hospital where she had been moved to after she was well enough to leave ITU and a ghost of a smile curved his lips when he found her dressed and sitting in a chair. He was relieved to see a faint tinge of colour on her cheeks, but she still looked as fragile as spun glass and his stomach twisted.

'You look better.' It was a lie but he suddenly didn't know what to say to her. The little scrap of life that neither he nor Sara had planned for her to conceive was gone. He did not know how she felt about the loss of their child, and he didn't want to face his own feelings. So he forced himself to smile as he picked up her holdall. 'Are you ready to come home?'

She avoided looking directly at him, and that was a bad sign. 'I'm not going to the penthouse with you.'

'I realise it holds bad memories. We can go somewhere else. I'll check with the doctor that you are okay to fly and we'll go to Eiríni.'

'No.' At last she did look at him and wiped away a

tear as it slid down her cheek. 'It's not the penthouse. I'm sad that I lost the baby, but we only knew I was pregnant for two weeks. I was just getting used to the idea of being a mother but now...that's not going to happen.' She took something out of her handbag and held out her hand to him. 'I need to give you this.'

He stared at her engagement ring sparkling in his palm and a nerve jumped in his cheek.

'Now there is no baby there is no reason for us to marry,' she said quietly.

Something roared inside Alekos. He felt unbalanced, as if the world had tilted on its axis and he was falling into a dark place. All he had thought about for the past days was Sara and the baby they had lost. *This* scenario had not occurred to him and he didn't know what to say or think or feel.

'There is no need for either of us to make hasty decisions. You've been through hell and need time to recuperate before we think about the future.'

She shook her head. '*We* don't have a future together. Your only reason for deciding to marry me was because I was pregnant with your child.'

'That's not strictly true. There were other reasons that are still valid even though there is no baby.'

'What reasons?' She stared at him and Alekos saw the sudden tension in her body and the faint betraying tremble of her lower lip. For a moment he almost gave in to the urge to put his arms around her and smell the vanilla scent of her hair. He was almost tempted to listen to the roaring inside him. But then he thought of Dimitri walking into the sea, throwing away his life for love, and the fortress walls closed around Alekos's heart.

'My position as chairman of GE will be strengthened

if I marry. The board members like and respect you—as I do. I value you, Sara. We are a good team and I am confident that if you were my wife you would run my home as efficiently as you ran my office.'

To his own ears his words sounded pompous and Sara gave an odd laugh. 'You make marriage sound like I would be your PA with a few extra perks.'

'Excellent perks,' he said drily. A lot of women would jump at the chance to live the wealthy lifestyle he was offering. 'You would not have to work and could study art or do whatever you want to do. And let's not forget sex.' He watched her pale cheeks flood with colour and was amazed she could blush when he knew her body as well as his own and had kissed every centimetre of her creamy skin. 'The sexual chemistry between us shows no sign of burning out.'

'And you resent it,' she said slowly. 'The marriage you described is not enough for me. I don't care about your money,' she said quickly before he could speak, 'and I agree the sex is great. But you would tire of me eventually. I was your PA for two years and I know the short lifespan of your interest in women.'

'What do you want, then?' he demanded, furious with her for reading him too well.

'The saddest thing is that you have to ask.' She stood up and gathered up her handbag. 'My friend Ruth is coming to pick me up and she's invited me to stay with her because my mother's house has now been sold.'

It hit Alekos then that she actually meant it and something akin to panic cramped in his gut. 'Sara, we can talk.'

'Until we're blue in the face,' she said flatly, 'but it won't change anything. I understand why you won't

allow anyone too close. I know you feel guilty because
you think you should have done more to help your
brother. But you can't live in the past for ever, Alekos.
Love isn't an enemy you have to fight and I don't believe Dimitri would have wanted you to live your life
without love.'

'Even though loving someone cost him his life?' Alekos said savagely.

'You don't know for sure that he did mean to end
his life. You told me you never talked about Dimitri's
death with the rest of your family. Maybe you should.
Because a life without love will make you as bitter and
unhappy as my mother was, and how I would become
if I married you.'

Her words stung him. 'I don't remember you being
unhappy when we were on Eiríni.' He pulled her into
his arms and sought her mouth. 'I made you happy,' he
muttered against her lips. 'Do you think you'll find this
passion with anyone else?'

He kissed her hard and his body jerked when he felt
her respond. She was a golden light in his life, and he
realised that almost from the first day she had started
working for him he had looked forward to her cheerful smile every morning and he'd felt comfortable with
her in a way he had never felt with other women. They
had been friends before they were lovers but she was
prepared to walk away from what they had because he
refused to put a label on what he felt for her.

He knew how to seduce her. He knew how to kiss
her with a deepening hunger so that she flattened out
her bunched fists on his chest and slid her arms up
around his neck. Her body melted into him and triumph

surged through him, spiking his already heated blood. She couldn't deny *this*.

He couldn't believe it when she wrenched her mouth from beneath his and pushed against his chest. He was unprepared for her rejection and dropped his arms to his sides as she stepped away from him. 'You want me,' he said harshly. 'We're good together, Sara, but I won't beg. If I walk away I won't come back. Ever.'

He held his breath as she stood on tiptoe and brushed her lips gently on his cheek. 'I hope that one day you will find the happiness you deserve. And I hope I will too. I can't settle for second best, Alekos.'

He froze. *Second best*. Was that what she thought of him? The same as his father had thought. *Theos*, she might as well have stabbed him through his heart. The pain in his chest felt as if she had.

Sara watched Alekos stride out of her hospital room and nearly ran after him. She sank down onto the bed as the enormity of what she had done drained the little strength she had in her legs after her ordeal of the ectopic pregnancy. The sense of loss that swept over her was almost unbearable.

When she'd regained consciousness and discovered she was lying in a hospital bed she had known immediately that her baby hadn't survived. The grief she felt was greater than anything she'd experienced. It was true she had only known for a few weeks that she was pregnant but there was a hollow space inside her and she felt as though her hopes for her future as a mother had been ripped from her as savagely as her child had been ripped from her body.

Now she had lost Alekos too. She would never see

him again, never feel his strong arms around her or feel him move inside her in the timeless dance of love. Because it wasn't love, she reminded herself. What she'd had with Alekos was wonderful sex that for him had been meaningless.

Much as she hated to acknowledge it, she had been just another mistress. The only difference between her and all the other countless women he'd had affairs with was that the board members of GE approved of her, which was why he had wanted to marry her despite her no longer being pregnant.

She knew she had done the right thing to turn him down. Her close brush with death when her tube had ruptured had shown her that life was too precious to waste a moment of it. There had been a moment when she'd thought Alekos was going to admit that he cared for her and she'd held her breath and hoped with all her heart, only to hear him say that he valued her in the same way that he might have said he valued a priceless painting or one of the flash superyachts his company was famous for building.

Once she would have been grateful for any crumb he offered her. She had been so lacking in self-confidence that she would have married him because she had adored him and didn't believe that a handsome, charismatic and sophisticated man such as Alekos could fall in love with his plain, frumpy secretary.

Meeting her father had made her feel like a whole person. Casting her mind back over the past months, she could see that she had taken more interest in her appearance because she felt more worthwhile, and maybe it was her new confidence that had attracted Alekos as much as her new, sexier clothes and hairstyle. But crucially she had forgotten that he'd once said love was simply a word used by poets and romantics to describe lust.

The sound of a deep male voice outside the door made her heart leap into her throat. But when she stepped into the corridor it was not Alekos standing in front of the nurses' station, arguing with a nurse and drawing attention from a crowd of curious onlookers.

'I don't care if my name is not on the visitor list,' Lionel Kingsley said loudly. 'Sara Lovejoy is my daughter and I have come to visit her.' He glanced round and his expression became concerned when he saw her. 'Sara, my dear, you should be resting.' He spoke briefly on his mobile phone as he walked over to her and Sara hurriedly pulled him into her room and shut the door.

'What are you doing here? There must be a dozen people who heard you say that I am your daughter.' She bit her lip. 'It's probably already on social media and once the press get hold of the story it will be headline news, especially as there is speculation that you will be the new Home Secretary in the Cabinet reshuffle.'

'None of that is important.' Lionel swept her into a bear hug. 'What matters is that you are safe and as well as can be expected after you nearly lost your life. Alekos phoned and told me what had happened, and how you lost your baby.' He squeezed her so hard that she felt breathless. 'I'm so sorry, Sara. For your loss, and also for my behaviour. Alekos used some very colourful language when he pointed out that I had failed you as a father twice. The first time by not being around when you were a child, and the second by not publicly acknowledging you as my daughter.'

'He told you that?' she said faintly.

'And a lot more. He reminded me I was lucky to have a beautiful, compassionate and loyal daughter. When he told me how you had almost died I realised how stupid and selfish I had been. I should have welcomed you unreservedly, and I'm sorry I didn't before now.'

'But what about Charlotte and Freddie?' Sara was reeling from hearing how Alekos had stood up for her to her father. 'How do you think they will take the news that I am their sister?'

'Why don't you ask them? Or one of them, at least,' Charlotte Kingsley said as she walked into the room. 'Freddie is in America, but he said to tell you that he knows who you remind him of now.' She smiled at Sara's startled expression. 'You and I do look remarkably alike and not only because we both have green eyes. All three of dad's offspring take after his side of the family, and Freddie agrees with me that we can't think of a nicer person to have as our sister.'

'I thought you would hate me,' Sara said unsteadily.

Charlotte clasped her hand. 'Why would we hate you? Nothing that happened in the past is your fault. I'm sad that I didn't know about you for twenty-five years, but now I hope you will be part of our family for ever…if you want to be.'

Sara glanced at her father. 'Aren't you worried that the scandal will affect your political career?'

Lionel shrugged. 'These things often blow over. I behaved badly towards your mother and my wife many years ago and the person who suffered most was you. Far more important than my career is my determination to try and make amends and be the father I should have been to you when you were growing up. And I'd like to start by taking you to my home in Berkshire so that you can recuperate, but of course I'll understand if you want to go home with Alekos.'

Her father looked puzzled. 'Actually, I assumed Alekos would be here. I know he refused to leave your bedside while you were in intensive care. And when he came to see me yesterday to tell me what he thought of me for treating you badly, he looked like he'd been to hell and back. But it's not surprising after he lost his child and could have lost you too. It's obvious how much he cares for you.'

Sara sat down heavily on the chair and buried her face in her hands. She felt as if she was on an emotional roller coaster from her intense sadness at losing her baby and the shock of realising how close she had come to losing her own life. She had rejected Alekos without considering his feelings about the loss of their child. Although her pregnancy had been in the early stages, it was likely that the trauma had reminded him of losing his brother when he was a teenager.

A sob escaped her and she felt a hand patting her shoulder. Charlotte—her sister—she thought emotively, pushed some tissues into her hand. 'Cry it out, Sara. You've been through a terrible experience and you need time to grieve for the baby.'

As Alekos did. But she knew he would bottle up his feelings like he had when Dimitri died. 'I think I've made a terrible mistake,' she choked. Alekos needed her but she had sent him away and her tears were for the baby, for her, but mainly for the man she would always love.

CHAPTER ELEVEN

ALEKOS HAD SPENT his childhood at his parents' house just outside Athens. As a boy he had spent hours playing on the private beach but after Dimitri died he had stopped going there.

He moved away from the window, where he had been watching huge waves crash onto the shore. The recent storm had made the sea angry and the heavy sky echoed his mood. He picked up his brother's death certificate from the desk in his father's study and read it once more before he looked at his mother.

'Why didn't you tell me Dimitri suffered a heart attack when he went swimming and that was why he drowned?'

'You never wanted to talk about him. If his name was mentioned by anyone you would leave the room. Your father and I were advised not to push you to discuss the accident but to wait for you to bring up the subject.'

She sighed. 'Dimitri was born with a small hole in his heart but later tests showed that the defect had healed by itself and it was not expected to cause problems as he grew up. Your brother was such a strong, athletic boy and your father and I more or less forgot that there had been the early problem. When we learned that Dimitri had suffered heart failure we felt guilty that we should have persuaded him to have more health checks. The reason why Dimitri drowned was something we could not bear to discuss with you and your sisters. Why does your brother's cause of death matter now, so many years later?'

Alekos swallowed hard. 'I believed for all those years that Dimitri took his own life. He was heartbroken when he found out his girlfriend had cheated on him and he told me he did not want to live without Nia.'

His mother frowned. 'I remember he was upset over a girl. Your father had arranged for him to go and work in the Miami office for a few months to help him get over her. You were not at home on that last evening and so you did not see how excited Dimitri was about the trip to America.' She looked intently at her youngest son. 'I'm quite certain your brother knew he had everything to live for. He often went swimming at night and told me I worried too much when I asked him not to go into the sea alone.'

'I blamed myself for not getting help for Dimitri after he told me he felt depressed,' Alekos said gruffly. 'I felt guilty that I hadn't saved him. I missed him so much but I didn't want to cry in front of anyone because I was fourteen, not a baby. The only way I could cope was by not talking about him.'

'Dimitri's death was fate,' his mother said gently. 'I wish I had known how you felt, but I'm afraid you take after your father in the respect of not discussing your feelings. Kostas believed he must be strong for the rest of the family, but losing Dimitri made him withdraw emotionally. I think he found it hard to show how much he loved you because he was afraid of losing another child and suffering the same pain and grief he'd felt when Dimitri died.' She wiped away a tear. 'Your father was very proud of you, you know. He admired your drive and determination to take GE forward.'

'I wish I had known that Bampás approved of my ideas. I regret I didn't talk about Dimitri with him. It might have helped both of us.'

His mother nodded. 'Honesty and openness are important in a relationship and you should remember that when you marry Sara.'

Alekos's jaw clenched. 'Sara ended our engagement because I can't give her what she wants.'

'Sara does not strike me as someone who craves material possessions.'

'She says she will only marry for love.'

'Well, what other reason is there for marriage?'

He frowned. 'I thought that you and Bampás had an arranged marriage?'

His mother laughed. 'Our parents thought so too. But Kostas and I had met secretly and fallen in love, and we engineered our so-called arranged marriage. Love is the only reason to marry. Why is it a problem? You love Sara, don't you?'

Alekos could not reply to his mother's question, although he suspected the answer was somewhere in the mess of emotions that had replaced the cool logic which had served him perfectly well for two decades.

'I understand why my father was scared to love after he lost a son,' he said. His voice sounded as if it had scraped over rusty metal. He had a flashback to when he had been in the hospital waiting room, praying harder than he'd prayed in his life that Sara's life would be saved. 'Love can hurt,' he said roughly.

'But it can also bring the greatest joy,' his mother said softly. 'I am glad I was blessed with Dimitri and it was better to have him for twenty-one years than not to have known him and loved him. The pain I felt when he died was terrible, but the happiness he gave me in his short life was far greater.'

It was a wonderful party, and she was absolutely having a brilliant time, Sara told herself firmly. She looked around the ballroom of the five-star hotel in Mayfair and recognised numerous celebrities who, like her, had been invited to the birthday celebrations of a famous music producer.

Since the news that she was the daughter of Lionel Kingsley, MP, had made the headlines a month ago, she had been on the guest list at many top social events with her half-brother and half-sister. She loved being part of a family and while she was staying at her father's beautiful house in Berkshire she'd grown close to Lionel, Charlotte and Freddie. They and her father had encouraged her to follow a different career path after she'd resigned from her position as Alekos's PA. She had started an art foundation course at college and her plan to go to university to study for an art degree helped to take her mind off the trauma of the ectopic pregnancy.

Long walks in the countryside and the companionship of family mealtimes had gradually enabled her to come to terms with the loss of her baby, although there would always be a little ache in her heart for the child she would never know. Getting over Alekos had so far proved more difficult, especially when she had told her father and siblings that she had broken off her relationship with him and they had asked if she was sure she had done the right thing.

Well, she was sure now, she thought dismally. Photos of Alekos at a film premiere with a busty blonde wrapped around him had featured on the front pages of all the tabloids. She was furious with herself that she'd wasted time worrying about him. Why, she'd even phoned him to check if he was okay because it had been his baby too. He hadn't answered her call or replied to the message she'd left him, and seeing the picture of him with his latest bimbo had forced her to accept that he had moved on with his life and she should do the same.

She was jolted from her thoughts by a sharp pain in her foot. 'Sorry—again,' the man she was dancing with said ruefully when she winced. 'That must be the third time I've trodden on your toes.'

'Fourth, actually.'

She hid her irritation with a smile. He had introduced himself as Daniel, 'I'm doing a bit of modelling but I really want to be an actor,' and he was very good-looking, although it was lucky he wasn't hoping for a career as a dancer, she mused. Unfortunately, his good looks were wasted on her. She wished her heart did skip a beat when he pulled her closer, but she felt nothing. Although she managed to put on a cheerful front, she missed Alekos terribly and couldn't stop thinking about him.

'Is there a reason why the tall guy over there is staring at me as if he's planning to murder me?' Daniel murmured. 'He's coming this way and I get the feeling it's time I made myself scarce.'

'Which guy...?' Sara felt her heart slam into her ribs when Alekos materialised at her side.

'I advise you to find another woman to dance with,' he growled to Daniel, who immediately dropped his hands from Sara as if she were highly contagious. But her attention wasn't on Daniel. Alekos swamped all of her senses and he was the only man in the ballroom.

He looked utterly gorgeous dressed in slim black trousers and a black shirt open at the throat to reveal a sprinkling of curling chest hairs. His hair was ruffled as if he'd been running his fingers through it—or someone else had, Sara thought darkly, remembering the photos of him with the blonde who'd been stuck to him with superglue. Temper rescued her from the ignominy of drooling over him.

'How dare you barge in and spoil my evening?' she snapped.

'I dare, Sara *mou*, because if I hadn't persuaded your pretty boy dance partner to back off I would have throttled him with my bare hands.' His dark eyes burned like hot embers and the tight grip of his hands on her waist warned her that he was furious. Well, that made two of them, she thought, glaring at him when she tried to pull away and he jerked her against his body. The feel of his hard thighs pressed close to hers was almost enough to make her melt.

'I am definitely not *your* Sara. Will you let go of me? You're making an exhibition of us.'

'I haven't even started,' he warned. 'You can walk out of the ballroom with me or I'll carry you out.'

She snapped her teeth together as if she would like to bite him, but to safeguard her dignity she allowed him to steer her out of the ballroom and across the hotel foyer to the lifts. 'Won't your girlfriend mind? Don't pretend you don't know who I mean. You must have seen the picture on the front page of this morning's papers of you and Miss Breast Implants.'

His puzzled expression cleared. 'Oh, you mean Charlene.'

'I don't read gossip columns so I don't know her name.'

'Charlene McCuskey is the wife of Warren McCuskey, who I'm sure you recall is buying *Artemis*. They are in London so that Warren can finalise the purchase, but he has come down with a virus and so he asked me to escort Charlene to a film premiere, which I dutifully did before I took her back to their hotel. Unsurprisingly, she is devoted to her billionaire husband,' he said sardonically.

'Oh, I see,' Sara muttered. Without fully realising what she was doing she'd followed Alekos into a lift, and as the doors closed and she was alone with him in the small space she had a horrible feeling that he saw way too much of her thoughts. 'Where are you taking me?'

'I'm staying at the hotel and we are going to my suite.'

'I don't want…'

'We need to talk.' Something in his expression made her heart give another painful jolt. The lift had mirrored walls, and her reflection showed her breasts rising and falling jerkily beneath her scarlet silk dress that she'd worn thinking the bright colour might lift her spirits. 'You look beautiful,' Alekos told her brusquely.

Her eyes flew to his face and after weeks of feeling nothing every nerve ending on her body was suddenly fiercely alive. The lift stopped, and as she followed him along the corridor and into his suite she wondered why she was putting herself through this. Seeing him again was going to make it so much harder to get over him.

'Would you like a drink?'

It would give her something to do with her hands. When she nodded he walked over to the bar, poured a measure of cassis into two tall glasses and topped them up with champagne. Sara remembered they had drunk Kir Royale the night they had become lovers on the yacht in Monaco. It seemed a lifetime ago.

'How are you?'

'Good,' she said huskily. It wasn't true, but she was working on it. 'It's been great getting to know Charlotte and Freddie. I feel very lucky that they and my father are part of my life.'

'I'm sure they feel lucky to have found you.' There was an odd note in his voice and, like in the lift, the indefinable expression in his eyes stirred feelings inside her that she told herself she must not feel.

'How about you?' She hesitated. 'I phoned you...but you didn't call back.'

'I was in Greece. I visited my mother and we talked about my brother.' He indicated for Sara to sit down on a sofa but she felt too edgy to sit, and he remained standing too. 'Dimitri died of a heart attack while he was swimming,' he told her abruptly. 'I finally read the coroner's report. My parents had their reasons for not talking about the cause of his death and I never spoke about Dimitri because I tried to block out my grief.'

'I'm glad you found out the truth at last and can stop blaming yourself,' she said softly. 'I hope you can put the past behind you and move on with your life.'

'Do you include yourself in my past and hope I will forget about you?'

She swallowed. Alekos had moved without her being aware of him doing so and he was standing so close that she could see the tiny lines around his eyes that suggested he hadn't been sleeping well. There were deeper grooves on either side of his mouth and she sensed he was as tense as she felt.

'I guess we both need to move forwards,' she said, aiming for a light tone. 'Make a fresh start.'

'What if I asked you to come back to me?'

Her heart missed a beat, but she shook her head. 'I couldn't be your PA now that we...' she coloured '...now that we have had a personal association.'

'A *personal association*?' he said savagely. '*Theos*, Sara, we created a child together.'

'*A child you didn't want*. Any more than you wanted to marry me.' She spun away from him, determined not to break down in front of him.

'That's not true on both counts. I did want to marry you. I didn't respond to your phone call because when you went to stay with your father after you left hospital, I agreed with Lionel to give you some space. You needed to recover from the ectopic and spend time with your new family.'

Sara shrugged to show she didn't care, even though she did desperately. Alekos frowned but continued, 'I also did what every bridegroom is expected to do and asked your father if he would allow me to marry you.'

Sara choked on her mouthful of champagne. '*You did what?*' She was so angry she wanted to hit him and for about twenty seconds she forgot that she wanted to kiss him. 'There is no way I would agree to marry you to keep the board members of GE happy.'

'Good, because that's a terrible reason for us to

marry,' he said calmly, although his eyes blazed with a fierce heat that melded Sara to the floor and stopped her rushing towards the door.

'I'm being serious.' She put her hands flat on his chest to stop him coming closer but he clasped her wrists and pulled her arms down, at the same time as he tugged her against him with a force that expelled the air from her lungs.

'So am I.' He stared at her intently and his jaw clenched when he saw the tears she was struggling to hold back. 'Why were you jealous when you saw the photo of me with Charlene?'

She flushed. 'I wasn't jealous.'

'Did you feel like I did tonight when I saw you dancing with that guy and I wanted to tear his head off?'

'Definitely not.' She didn't know what game of refined torture Alekos was playing but it had to stop before the intoxicating warmth of his body pressed up against hers and ruined her for ever.

'Liar,' he taunted. 'Were you jealous because you love me?'

She could deny it but what would be the point? She couldn't fight him or herself any more, and Sara knew she would be his mistress if he asked her because she'd learned that life was too short to turn down the chance to be with him, even though he would break her heart when he ended their affair.

But she still had her pride and her eyes flashed with green fire. '*Yes*, I love you. I've loved you for ever, even though you are the most arrogant man I've ever known.'

'But I am the only man you have ever known intimately, arrogant or not,' he said softly, his mouth curving in a crooked smile that tugged on Sara's heart. He sounded strange, as if his throat was constricted, and her eyes widened in disbelief when she saw that his lashes were wet.

'Alekos?' she whispered.

'Sara *mou*...' He held her so tight that she felt the thunder of his heart. '*S'agapo.* I love you so much.' He framed her face with his hands that were shaking. 'When I watched your life ebbing away in the ambulance on the way to hospital I was terrified I would lose you. And I realised then that I had tried hard *not* to fall in love with you because of fear. I associated love with the loss and pain that I felt after Dimitri died.'

'That's not surprising,' she said shakily. 'You were at an impressionable age when he died, and your brother was your best friend.'

'We became friends when you worked for me, didn't we, Sara? I liked you and I respected you when you put me in my place. I felt closer to you than I'd ever felt with any of my mistresses. But one day I walked into my office and I was blown away by a gorgeous sexy brunette. You can imagine my shock when I discovered it was you.'

She flushed. 'Before that day you didn't notice your frumpy PA.'

'I did notice you. Often I would find myself thinking about a funny remark you'd made, and I appreciated your fierce intelligence and your advice on how to handle work issues. I almost resented you when you made me desire you too. I knew I was in danger of falling in love with you and I told myself that once we were lovers my interest in you would fade. Instead, it grew stronger every day and night that we were together. When you

told me you were pregnant I seized the excuse to marry
you without having to admit how I felt about you.'

How he felt about her. Sara bit her lip and told herself it was too good to be true. 'You said love is a word
that poets use to describe lust. Are you sure you haven't
got the two mixed up?'

'I don't blame you for doubting me, *kardia mou.*
That means my heart, and I love you with all my heart.'

Sara's head advised caution but her heart was desperate to believe that, incredible as it seemed, Alekos was
looking at her with adoration in his eyes. She caught
her breath when he stroked his finger gently down her
cheek.

'Will you marry me, my Sara, for no other reason
than you are the love of my life?'

That was the moment she knew she should have lis-
tened to the warning that it was all too good to be true.
Carefully she eased out of his arms and closed her eyes
to blot out the sudden haggard look on his face. 'I can't.'

'*Theos*, Sara, I will do whatever it takes to prove
to you that I love you.' His voice cracked. 'Please believe me.'

'I do. And I love you. But you need an heir to one
day run GE, and there is a strong chance I won't be able
to give you a child because I lost one tube and there is
a higher risk I could have another ectopic pregnancy.'

He caught her to him and buried his face in her hair.
'Then we won't have children. There's no way I will
risk your life. I need *you*,' he told her fiercely. 'Nothing else is important. Whatever the future holds, I want
us to share it together, the ups and the downs, for the
rest of our lives.'

He tightened his arms around her so that she was

aware of his hard thigh muscles pressed against her. 'My body knew the truth before I was ready to accept it,' he said roughly. 'When we made love it was so much more than great sex.'

Joy fizzed inside Sara like champagne bubbles exploding. Hearing Alekos say he loved her wiped away the pain and misery of the past weeks and the future shimmered on the horizon like a golden sun. 'Mmm, but it was great sex, wasn't it?' Her smile was wicked and adoring. 'I think you should remind me.'

His laughter rumbled through her and the unguarded expression in his eyes stole her breath even before his mouth did the same as he claimed her lips and kissed her so thoroughly, so *lovingly*, that she was trembling when he finally lifted his head.

'I'd better warn you that this is the honeymoon suite and the staff have really gone to town,' he murmured. 'There are rose petals everywhere in the bedroom.'

Alekos had been right about the rose petals, Sara discovered when he carried her into the bedroom and laid her on the bed, adorned with fragrant red petals. He undressed her slowly, kissing each part of her body that he revealed, and when he removed her knickers and pressed his mouth to her feminine heat she told him she loved him, loved him. She repeated the words when he thrust into her so deeply that he filled her and he made love to her with all the love in his heart.

It was as wonderful as she remembered and more beautiful than she could ever have dreamed because this time Alekos didn't just show her he loved her; he told her in a mixture of English and Greek.

'Will you let me love you for ever, and will you love

me?' he murmured as he drew her close and they relaxed in the sweet aftermath of loving.

'I will,' Sara promised him and she meant the words with her heart and soul.

They were married three months later on Christmas Eve, in a church decorated with holly and ivy and fragrant red roses, and filled with their families and friends. Sara wore a white satin and lace gown and carried a bouquet of white lilies. Alekos looked stunning in a dark grey suit, but it was the look in his eyes as he watched his bride walk down the aisle towards him that made his mother and sisters wipe away tears. Sara's father walked proudly beside her to meet her husband-to-be, and her half-sister was her maid of honour.

After the reception at Lionel Kingsley's home in Berkshire, the happy couple flew to South Africa for their honeymoon. 'Somewhere hot where you can wear less clothes,' Alekos had stated when Sara had asked him where he wanted to go.

As it turned out, neither of them got dressed very often during the three weeks they stayed in a private bungalow at a luxury beach resort, a fact that Sara later accounted for her pregnancy that was confirmed a month after they returned to London. It was an anxious time until an early scan showed that her pregnancy was normal and they watched the tiny beating heart of their baby with hope in their hearts.

Theodore Dimitri Gionakis, to be known as Theo, arrived in the world two weeks early with a minimum of fuss and instantly became the centre of his parents' world.

'Love changes everything,' Alekos said one evening

as he held his son in the crook of one arm and slid his other arm around his wife's waist. 'You changed me, Sara *mou*. You showed me how to let love into my heart and now it's there to stay for ever.'

'For ever sounds wonderful,' she told him, and then she kissed him and no further words were necessary.

* * * * *

If you enjoyed this story, here are some more great reads from Chantelle Shaw for you to try!

TRAPPED BY VIALLI'S VOWS
MASTER OF HER INNOCENCE
MISTRESS OF HIS REVENGE
A BRIDE WORTH MILLIONS
SHEIKH'S FORBIDDEN CONQUEST

Available now!

MILLS & BOON®

MODERN™

POWER, PASSION AND IRRESISTIBLE TEMPTATION

A sneak peek at next month's titles...

In stores from 9th February 2017:

- **Secrets of a Billionaire's Mistress** – Sharon Kendrick
- **The Innocent's Secret Baby** – Carol Marinelli
- **A Debt Paid in the Marriage Bed** – Jennifer Hayward
- **Pursued by the Desert Prince** – Dani Collins

In stores from 23rd February 2017:

- **Claimed for the De Carrillo Twins** – Abby Green
- **The Temporary Mrs Marchetti** – Melanie Milburne
- **The Sicilian's Defiant Virgin** – Susan Stephens
- **The Forgotten Gallo Bride** – Natalie Anderson

Just can't wait?
Buy our books online before they hit the shops!
www.millsandboon.co.uk

Also available as eBooks.

MILLS & BOON®

EXCLUSIVE EXTRACT

Raul Di Savo desires more than Lydia Hayward's
body—his seduction will stop his rival buying her!
Raul's expert touch awakens Lydia to irresistible
pleasure, but his game of revenge forces
Lydia to leave... until an unexpected
consequence binds them forever!

Read on for a sneak preview of
THE INNOCENT'S SECRET BABY

Somehow Lydia was back against the wall with Raul's
hands either side of her head.

She put her hands up to his chest and felt him solid
beneath her palms and she just felt him there a moment
and then looked up to his eyes.

His mouth moved in close and as it did she stared
right into his eyes.

She could feel heat hover between their mouths in a
slow tease before they first met.

Then they met.

And all that had been missing was suddenly there.

Yet, the gentle pressure his mouth exerted, though
blissful, caused a mire of sensations until the gentleness
of his kiss was no longer enough.

A slight inhale, a hitch in her breath and her lips
parted, just a little, and he slipped his tongue in.

The moan she made went straight to his groin.

At first taste she was his and he knew it for her hands

moved to the back of his head and he kissed her as hard back as her fingers demanded.

More so even.

His tongue was wicked and her fingers tightened in his thick hair and she could feel the wall cold and hard against her shoulders.

It was the middle of Rome just after six and even down a side street there was no real hiding from the crowds.

Lydia didn't care.

He slid one arm around her waist to move her body away from the wall and closer into his, so that her head could fall backwards.

If there was a bed, she would be on it.

If there was a room they would close the door.

Yet there wasn't and so he halted them, but only their lips.

Their bodies were heated and close and he looked her right in the eye. His mouth was wet from hers and his hair a little messed from her fingers.

Don't miss
THE INNOCENT'S SECRET BABY,
By Carol Marinelli

Available March 2017
www.millsandboon.co.uk

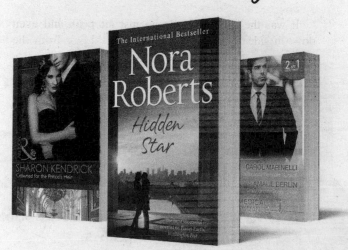